"So you've done ~~what I~~
asked of you.**

"You've watched out for me, employed my dad.
You can go on with your life now and not worry
about me."

"It's not that easy," Gabriel said with reluctance.
"Your kids have gotten under my skin."

Laura looked at him. "What do you mean?"

"See, this is the part I wasn't expecting," he said,
realizing all of a sudden what he hadn't been
able to put into words before. "I didn't expect to
find myself caring about your children."

Her face was a blank he couldn't read. Gabriel
knew he had headed into deep water, and there
was no going back to shore. "It's okay," he said,
steeling his heart. "I just find myself thinking
about them...and even if I wanted to leave town,
I don't think I could leave *them*."

Dear Reader,

We hope you already know that Harlequin American Romance publishes heartwarming stories about the comforts of home and the joys of family. To celebrate our 25th year, we're pleased to present a special miniseries that sings the praises of the home state of six different authors, and shares the many trials and delights of being a parent.

Welcome to the first book in our THE STATE OF PARENTHOOD miniseries, *Texas Lullaby*. Tina Leonard lives in Texas and has written an irresistible story about a man who reluctantly returns to his family ranch, and falls in love with a young widow and her two adorable children. While he's trying to win over a potential wife, he truly learns what it means to be a father!

Watch for five more books in the series, coming out one per month. In July, Lynnette Kent tells the story of a woman who is reunited with a former teacher—and former crush—who is now a widower with a young son. The Smoky Mountains of North Carolina set a magical backdrop to this touching romance in *Smoky Mountain Reunion*. Watch for more stories by authors Cathy McDavid, Tanya Michaels, Margot Early and Laura Marie Altom.

We hope these romantic stories inspire you to celebrate where you live—because any place you raise a child is home.

Wishing you happy reading,

Kathleen Scheibling
Senior Editor
Harlequin American Romance

Tina Leonard
TEXAS LULLABY

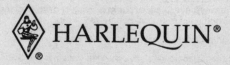

HARLEQUIN®

TORONTO • NEW YORK • LONDON
AMSTERDAM • PARIS • SYDNEY • HAMBURG
STOCKHOLM • ATHENS • TOKYO • MILAN • MADRID
PRAGUE • WARSAW • BUDAPEST • AUCKLAND

ISBN-13: 978-0-373-75217-1
ISBN-10:   0-373-75217-2

TEXAS LULLABY

Copyright © 2008 by Tina Leonard.

Recipes have not been tested by Harlequin Enterprises Limited. Harlequin Enterprises Limited accepts no responsibility for any injury, damage or loss resulting from the use of the recipes contained herein.

This edition published by arrangement with Harlequin Books S.A.

® and TM are trademarks of the publisher. Trademarks indicated with ® are registered in the United States Patent and Trademark Office, the Canadian Trade Marks Office and in other countries.

www.eHarlequin.com

Printed in U.S.A.

ABOUT THE AUTHOR

Tina Leonard loves to laugh, which is one of the many reasons she loves writing Harlequin American Romance books. In another lifetime, Tina thought she would be single and an East Coast fashion buyer forever. The unexpected happened when Tina met Tim again after many years—she hadn't seen him since they'd attended school together from first through eighth grade. They married, and now Tina keeps a close eye on her school-age children's friends! Lisa and Dean keep their mother busy with soccer, gymnastics and horseback riding. They are proud of their mom's "kissy books" and eagerly help her any way they can. Tina hopes that readers will enjoy the love of family she writes about in her books. A reviewer once wrote, "Leonard had a wonderful sense of the ridiculous," which Tina loved so much she wants it for her epitaph. Right now, however, she's focusing on her wonderful life and writing a lot more romance! You can visit her at www.tinaleonard.com.

Books by Tina Leonard

To my sister, Kimmie, who is simply my star,
and Lisa and Dean-O, my best friends,
and Kathleen Scheibling, who believes in my work,
and my gal pals, who are always there for me.

Chapter One

What doesn't kill a man makes him stronger
—Josiah Morgan's parting advice to his
teenage sons when they walked out of his life.

The four Morgan brothers shared an unspoken belief, if nothing else: stubbornness equaled strength. A man who didn't have "stubborn" etched into his bones hadn't yet grown into big boots.

Some people used the word *jackasses* to describe the family of four brothers, but the Morgans preferred to think of themselves as independent loners. It was common for them to be approached by women who wanted to relieve their "loneliness." The Morgans had no problem breaking with their routine for beautiful women bent on their relief.

Fortunately, most people in Union Junction, Texas, understood that a solitary way of life was a good thing, if it was lived by choice. The Morgan brothers were moving to the area not by choice, but for two different reasons. The first was continued solitude, which had been confirmed by some family acquaintances, the Jeffersons. Men after their own heart, the Jeffersons weren't loners, but they hadn't exactly been hanging out in bars every night sobbing about their sad lives before they'd all found the religion of love. They appreciated the need to be left the hell alone.

Yet the need for peace and quiet was just a cover for the real reason Gabriel Morgan had come home. This was about money. He stared at the two-story sprawling farmhouse set amongst native pecan trees and shouldered by farmland. For this house, this land, the Morgans were called to relocate to the Morgan Ranch near Union Junction. The first thing the brothers had all agreed on in years was that none of them was too happy about finding themselves the keeper of a large ranch. Five thousand acres as well as livestock—what the hell were they supposed to do with it? This was Pop's place. Light-footed Pop and his far-flung dreams, buying houses and land like he was buying up parts of earth to keep him alive and vital.

Pop was the true jackass.

Selling the ranch had been the first thing on Gabriel's mind, and he was pretty certain his brothers had the same idea. But no, Pop was too wily for that. Knowing full well his four sons weren't close, he'd come up with a brilliant plan to stick them all under one roof on acres and acres of loneliness where no one could witness the fireworks.

Pop was in Europe right now, in a new stone castle he'd bought in Pzenas, no doubt laughing his ass off at what he'd wrought. Oh, he couldn't buy just any old French countryside farmhouse—he'd bought an eighteen hundred Templar's commandery for a cool four million. It wasn't in the best of shape but just his style, he'd told his sons in the letters they'd each received outlining his wishes. Three floors, ten bedrooms, eight baths, plenty of room should they all ever decide to visit. It even had its own chapel, and he'd be in that chapel praying for them every day.

Gabriel doubted the prayers would help. Pop would be praying for family harmony, and truthfully, some growth in the family tree, some tiny feet to run on the floors of the stone castle, sweet angelic voices to learn how to say Grandpop in French. *Grand-père*.

Like hell. Family expansion wasn't on Gabriel's mind. He was looking for peace and quiet in this rural town, and he was going to get it. He'd live in the house just as his father had decreed, for the year he'd specified, take his part of the bribe money—money was always involved with Pop—and leave no different than he was today. Except he'd be a million dollars richer.

Easy pickings.

Gabriel would take the money. As for the unspoken part of the deal…. The pleasure of putting one over on his father, spitting in his eye, so to speak, would be a roundabout kick from one jackass to another. Pop hadn't said his sons had to be close-bonded Templar knights; he'd just stated they had to live in the house for a year. Like a family.

He could do that—if for no other reason than to show the old man he hadn't fazed Gabriel in the least.

"Hi!"

He turned to see a woman waving to him from a car

window. She parked, got out and handed him a freshly baked cherry pie.

"Welcome to Union Junction, stranger." Her blue eyes gleamed at him; her blond hair swung in a braid. "My name's Mimi Jefferson. I'm from the Double M ranch, once known as Malfunction Junction. I'm Mason's wife. And also the sheriff."

"Hello, Mimi." He'd met Mason months ago through Pop's business dealings, and Mason's wonderful wife had often been mentioned. "Thanks for the pie."

"No problem." She glanced at the farmhouse. "So what do you think of it? Hasn't changed much since you were last here."

Pop had made some additions to the house, rendering it more sprawling than Gabriel thought necessary. He'd added more acreage, too, but that was his dad's agenda. Always the grand visionary. "I haven't been inside."

She smiled. "It needs work."

That he could see from the outside. "I noticed."

"Should keep you real busy."

He nodded. "Seems that was my dad's plan."

She laughed. "Your father fit in real well here in Union Junction. I'm sure you will, too."

He didn't need to, wouldn't be here long enough to put down deep roots.

"By the way, I believe the ladies will be stopping by with some other goodies. We figured your dad left the fridge pretty empty when he went to France."

"The ladies?"

"You'll see." With a cryptic smile, she got into the

truck. "I'll tell Mason you'll be by to see him when you've settled in."

That meant it was time to head into the old hacienda of dread and bar the door. He had no desire to be the target of gray-haired, well-meaning church ladies toting fried chicken. "Thanks again for the pie."

She waved at him and drove off. Gabriel dug into his pocket for the key marked Number Four—he supposed that was because he was the fourth son or maybe because his father had four keys made—and headed toward the wraparound porch. It groaned under his weight, protesting his presence.

Then he heard a sound, like the growing din of a schoolyard at recess. As a code breaker for the Marines, he was tuned to hear the slightest bit of noise, and could even decipher murmured language. But what assaulted his ears wasn't trying to be secretive in any way. He watched as ten vehicles pulled into the graveled drive. His jaw tensed as approximately twenty women and children hopped out of the cars and trucks, each bearing a sack. Not just a covered dish or salad bowl, but a bag, clearly destined for him.

He was going to go crazy—and get fat in the process.

"We're the welcoming committee." A pretty blonde smiled at him as she approached the porch. "Don't be scared."

She'd nailed his emotion.

"I'm Laura Adams," she said. "These ladies—most of us—are from the hair salon, bakery, et cetera, in town. We formed the Union Junction Welcoming Committee some time ago after we received such a warm greeting when we arrived in this town. Many of us weren't raised in Union Junction. Our turn to do a good deed, you might say."

Except he didn't want the deed done to *him*. She smelled nice, though. Her voice was soft and pleasant and he liked the delicate frosting of freckles across her nose and cheeks. Big blue eyes gazed at him with a warmth he couldn't return at the moment.

The porch shook under his feet with the sound of more approaching women. He hadn't taken his eyes off Laura, for reasons he couldn't quite explain to himself. She opened her pretty pink lips to say more, introduce all her gift-bearing friends, when suddenly something wrapped itself around his thigh.

Glancing down, he saw a tiny towhead comfortably smiling up at him. "Daddy," she said, hugging his leg for all she was worth. "Daddy."

For the first time in his life, including the time he'd temporarily lost part of his hearing from an underwater mine explosion near a sub he'd been monitoring, he felt panic. But the women laughed, and Laura didn't seem embarrassed as she disengaged her daughter from his leg.

"Oh, sweetie, he might be a daddy, or he will be one day. Can you say Mr. Morgan?"

The child smiled at him beatifically, completely convinced that the world was a wonderful, happy place. "Morgan," she said softly.

So he'd be Morgan, just like Pop. He could remember people yelling his father's name, cursing his father's name, cheering his father's name. It was always something along the lines of either "Morgan, you jackass!" or "Morgan, you old dog!"

It didn't feel as bad as he thought it might. Gabriel wondered where the child's father was, and then decided it was none of his business. "I should invite you in," he said reluctantly to the gathering at large, his gaze on Laura. He could tell by their instant smiles that being invited in was exactly what they wanted. "Too hot in June to keep ladies on the porch. We can all see the new place at the same time and make some introductions."

"You haven't been inside your home yet?" Laura asked. "Mimi said she thought you might have arrived later than you planned."

"Tell me something," he said as he worked at the lock on the front door. The lock obviously hadn't been used in a long time and didn't want to move. "I'd heard Union Junction was great for peace and quiet. Is this one of those places where everybody knows everybody's business?"

That made everyone laugh. Not him—for Gabriel it was a serious question.

"Yes," Laura said. "That's one of the best parts of our town. Everyone cares about everybody."

Great. The lock finally gave in to his impatient twisting of key Number Four and he swung the door open. The first thing he realized was how hot the house was—like an oven.

The smell was the next thing to register. Musty, unused, closed-up. The ladies peered around his shoulders to the dark interior.

"Girls, we've got our work cut out for us," an older lady pronounced.

"That won't be necessary," Gabriel said as they brushed past him. Laura smiled at him, swinging her grocery sack to the opposite hip and taking her daughter's hand in hers.

"It's necessary," she said. "They can clean this place so fast it'll make your head spin. Besides, we've seen worse. Not much worse, of course. But your father's been gone a long time. Almost six months." She smiled kindly. "Frankly, we expected you a lot sooner."

"I wasn't in a hurry to get here." Neither were any of his brothers. During their curt e-mail transmissions, exchanged since their father's letter had been delivered to them, Dane had said he might swing by in January if he'd finished with his Texas Ranger duties by then, Pete said he might make it by February—depending upon the secret agent assignments he couldn't discuss—and Jack hadn't answered at all. Jack was the least likely of them all to give a damn about Pop, the ranch, or a million dollars.

His chicken brothers were making excuses, putting off the inevitable—except for Jack, who really was the wild card.

"Well, we're glad you're here now." She didn't seem to notice his grimness as she set her grocery sack on the counter. "Hope you like chicken, baby peas and rice."

"You don't have to do that." He heard the sound of a vacuum start up somewhere in the house, and windows opening. The fragrance of lemon oil began to waft from one of the rooms. The little girl clung to her mom, her eyes watching Gabriel's every move. "Really, I'm not hungry, and your little girl probably needs to be at home in bed." It was six o'clock—what time did children go to bed, anyway? He and his brothers had a strict bedtime of nine o'clock when they were kids, which they'd always ignored. Pop never came up the stairs to check on them, and they used a tree branch outside the house to cheat their curfew. Then one year, Pop sawed off the limb, claiming the old live oak was too close to the roof. They devised a rope ladder which they flung out on grappling hooks whenever they had a yen to meet up with girls or camp in the woods.

Or watch Jack practice at the forbidden rodeo in the fields lit only by the moon.

"Oh, Penny's fine. Don't worry about her. You're always happy, aren't you, Penny?"

Penny beamed at Gabriel. "Morgan," she murmured in a small child's breathy recitation. He felt his heart flip over in his chest as he returned the child's gaze. *Heartburn. I'm getting heartburn at the age of twenty-six.*

"I have a smaller version of Penny who is being watched for me right now." Laura smiled proudly as she unloaded the grocery sacks the ladies had loaded onto the kitchen counter. "Perrin is nine months old, and looks just like his father. You love your baby brother, don't you, Penny?" She looked down at her child, who nodded, though she didn't break her stare from Gabriel.

Gabriel felt his heart sink strangely in his chest. This woman was married, apparently happily so.

He was an idiot, and probably horny. The house was swarming with women and he had to get the preliminary hots for a married mom.

Good thing his yen was in the early stages—one

pretty face could replace another easily enough. "Listen, I don't want to be rude, but I just got in. I appreciate you and your friends trying to help, but—"

"But you would rather be alone."

He nodded.

"I understand." She flicked the oven on warm and slid the casserole inside. "I would, too, if I was you."

She knew nothing about him. He decided a reply wasn't needed.

"You know, I really liked your father," she said, hesitating. She stared at him with eyes he felt tugging at his desire. "I hated to see Mr. Morgan go."

"Josiah," he murmured.

"I didn't call him by his first name."

He shrugged. "You didn't know him too well, then."

"Because I didn't call him by his name or because I liked him?"

He looked at her, thinking *both, lady*.

"Mr. Morgan was fond of my children."

His radar went on alert. Here came the your-father-wants-you-to-settle-down chorus. He steeled himself.

She ran a gentle hand through Penny's long fine hair. "Of course, he dreamed of having his own grandchildren."

Gabriel frowned. That topic was none of her business. His family was too raw a subject for him to discuss with a stranger.

"You're going to hear this sooner or later." She gazed at him suddenly with clear, determined focus. "I'd rather you hear it from me."

He shrugged. "I'm listening." He reminded himself

that whatever she had to say didn't matter to him. What Pop had meant to the town of Union Junction was not his concern.

"Your father put a hundred thousand dollars into a trust for my children."

She'd caught his attention. Not because of the amount, but because Pop had to have lost his mind to have gone that soft. Pop was as miserly as he was stubborn, even complaining over church donations. All he was interested in was himself.

Or at least that had been the Pop of Gabriel's youth.

Truthfully, it astonished him that this tiny woman had the nerve to tell him she'd managed to wheedle money out of his father. Maybe Pop had finally begun to crack, all the years of selfishness taking their toll. More importantly, Laura was obviously the kind of woman with whom Gabriel should exercise great distance and caution. "Congratulations," he finally said, trying not to smirk. "A hundred grand is a nice chunk of change."

"Each."

He stared at her. "Each?"

"Each child got their own trust. Penny and Perrin both received a hundred thousand dollars. Your father said it wasn't a lot, but he wanted them to have something later in their lives. He doesn't want them to know about his gift, though, not until they're grown up." She smiled, and it seemed to Gabriel that her expression was sad. "They won't even remember him, then."

He had no idea what the hell to say to this woman. He was suspicious. He was dumbstruck. Perhaps he was even a little envious that she'd gained some type of affection in his father's heart, when he and his brothers had struggled for years and had received none.

She picked up Penny. "I just thought you should know."

He watched as she turned, heading for the front door. Over her mother's shoulder, Penny watched him with wistful eyes. What had been the relationship between Pop and Laura that such an astonishing gift would be given to her kids?

He could remember a cold, wet night in Poland, hunched behind a snowbank, listening to a radio he'd held with frozen fingers to pick up conversation in a bedroom in Gdańsk. He'd retrieved the information he'd needed, turned it in and got cleared to return home. Chilled, he'd called his father, thinking maybe his soul could use a good thawing and their relationship a delayed shot of warmth. He was young, idealistic, mostly broke, lonely. Damned cold in every area of his life.

He needed a bus ticket from the base, he'd told his father. The military would get him stateside, but he only had a few zloty in his pocket.

Pop had told him not to come crying to him for money. He said the greatest gift he could ever give him was the knowledge of how to stand on his own two feet.

That was ten years ago, and he could still hear the sound of the receiver slamming in his ear. He followed behind Laura, catching up to open the front door for her. "You must have meant a lot to my father."

She turned, slowly, her gaze meeting his, questioning. In a split second, she got the gist of his unspoken assumption. "Your reputation preceded you," she said softly. "You really are a jackass."

The door slammed behind her. Gabriel nodded to himself, silently agreeing with her assessment. Then he went to shoo his well-meaning friends out of the house he didn't want.

Chapter Two

Laura returned to her house, steaming. She put Penny down on the sofa and went to find Mimi, whom she could hear quietly singing to Perrin in the back of the house. "Thank you for watching my little man, Mimi." She looked down into the crib at her baby, and all the tension flowed from her.

Together they walked from the nursery. "So what did you think of Gabriel Morgan?" Mimi asked.

"Not much. He thinks I sucked up to his father to weasel money out of him." Laura shrugged her shoulders. "He's everything Mr. Morgan said he was. Cocky, brash, annoying."

Mimi laughed. "Not a man's best qualities. Wasn't he nice at all? He just seemed sort of shy to me."

Laura went to fix them both an iced tea. "I suppose I compare every man to my husband." Her gaze was reluctantly drawn to the framed, fingerprint-covered photo of Dave. Penny liked to look at the picture of her father, enjoyed hearing stories about him.

Dave had been such a kind man. Warm. Funny. Easy

to talk to. Nothing like the man she'd met today. Laura wrinkled her nose and tried not to think so tears wouldn't spring into her eyes. Heaven only knew Dave had his moments; he was no angel. They'd had their spats. But he'd been her first love and that counted for so much. It had been such a shock to lose him.

At least she had his children.

"I suppose it would be hard for me not to compare every man to Mason." Mimi smiled. "No one would measure up."

Laura nodded, appreciating her friend's understanding.

"Some would say there never was a tougher nut to crack than Mason Jefferson."

"Really?" Laura found that hard to believe. Mason loved his wife, loved his kids. Was always looking at Mimi, or holding her hand.

"Suffice it to say he was really difficult to get to the altar. Sometimes I even wondered why I wanted him there." Mimi laughed. "Talk about stubborn and hard to get along with."

"Dave was easy," Laura murmured. "Don't get me wrong, I'm not looking to replace Dave in my life at all. But I was hoping for a connection with Gabriel, something like the one I'd had with his father. I miss the old gentleman." She smiled sadly at Mimi. "I can't understand why his boys don't want to be close with him."

"Mr. Morgan was a different person with us than he was with his sons. They say people show themselves differently to everyone, and we probably saw his best side. He was a good man."

"Obviously his sons believe they understand him better, and they probably do." She and Mimi moved to the kitchen table. Penny came into the kitchen and crawled into her mother's lap. Laura handed her a vanilla wafer from a box left out on the table since yesterday. "I swear I do keep house. We don't always have food left out from the day before." She glanced at the sink where the pots were piled up from making the welcome meal for Gabriel.

"Try living in a house where grown men come and go all the time. They make a bigger mess than the kids." Mimi sipped her tea. "I'll help you clean it up in a bit."

Laura shook her head, appreciating the offer but not wanting the help. She didn't mind washing dishes. It was soothing to have her hands in warm dishwater, and somehow comforting to submerge dirty dishes in suds and then pull them gleaming from the water. "I didn't want him to misunderstand my relationship with his father."

Mimi nodded. "Men don't always temper their thoughts before they speak. Anyway, nobody tells Josiah Morgan what to do. Gabriel knows that."

Gabriel, too, struck Laura as the kind of man willing to fight any battle life threw at him.

"Besides, it's really none of Gabriel's business."

That was also true. She'd only told him about his father's gift to her children because she wanted him to know up front. "Okay, I give up on being mad. It's a waste of time."

Mimi got up from the table. "Let's wash these dishes."

"No, you go on home to your family. You've done enough for me, Mimi. I really appreciate you watching Perrin so he could nap."

"Did the doctor say how long it would take for the medicine to do some good?"

Perrin had colic, long bouts at night that worried Laura. Someone had suggested that the colic was stress-induced, and that Perrin was sensing his mother's sadness. It had been a shock when Dave had died, and she certainly had grieved—was still grieving—but it was an additional guilt that she was causing her son's pain. "The doctor said babies sometimes go through colic. The medicine might help, and putting him on a different formula. Or he could grow out of it."

Mimi patted her hand. "I'll come by to see you later at the school."

Laura nodded. "I'd like that."

She closed the door behind Mimi. Penny handed her a vanilla wafer, and for the first time that day, Laura felt content.

ON FRIDAY NIGHT, THREE days later, Gabriel finally drove into the small town of Union Junction. He could see what had drawn his father to this place. For one thing, it looked like a melding of the old West and a Norman Rockwell card. There was a main street where families were enjoying a warm June stroll, ice-cream cones or sodas in hand. A kissing booth sat in front of a bakery. Other booths lined the street in front of various shops.

He glanced at the kissing booth again, caught by a glimpse of blond hair and the long line outside the booth. All the booths had lines, but none as long as the kissing booth, which Gabriel figured was probably appropriate. If he was offered the choice of getting a kiss or throwing rings over a bottle, he'd definitely take the kiss.

"What's going on?" he asked a young cowboy at the back of the line.

"Town fair." The young man grinned at him. "You're Morgan, aren't you?"

He looked at him. "Aren't you too young to be buying kisses?"

He got a laugh for that. "Get in line and spend a buck, Mr. Morgan."

"Why?" He wasn't inclined to participate in the fun of a town fair. He'd just been looking around, trying to figure out why Pop had settled near here, trying to stave off some boredom.

"We're raising money for the elementary school. Need more desks. The town is certainly growing."

"Shouldn't the town be paying for that from taxes or something?"

"We like to do some recreational fund-raising, too."

Gabriel reluctantly fell into line. "So who are we kissing?"

"Laura Adams."

"We can't kiss her!" He had to admit the idea was inviting, but he also wanted to jerk the young man out of line—and every other man, too.

The line kept growing behind him.

"Why not?" His companion appeared puzzled.

Gabriel frowned. "She's married. And she's a mom."

The young man laughed. "Mimi Jefferson was working the booth an hour ago. It's the only time any of us can get near Mimi without getting our tails kicked by Mason, so most of us went through twice."

Gabriel's frown deepened.

"It's for a good cause," his new friend said. "Besides which, Laura's not married anymore."

Gabriel's mood lifted slightly. He felt his boots shuffling closer to the booth behind his talkative friend. "She's not?"

"Nah. Her husband died shortly after she gave birth to Perrin." His friend looked at him with surprise. "You should know all this. Your dad loved Laura's kids. Said they were probably the only—"

"I know. I know. Jeez." Gabriel rubbed at his chin, trying to decide if he liked how quickly the line was moving. And the young man was right. The gentlemen were leaving the line to catcalls and whistles and hurrying to the back of the line for another kiss. It was a never-ending kiss line of rascals. "I'm pretty sure I don't belong here."

"No better way to get to know people," his friend said cheerfully. "My name's Buck, by the way."

"Hi, Buck." He absently shook his hand. "I guess kissing's as good a way as any to get to know someone." He supposed he should get to know Laura better since they sort of had a connection.

Buck stared at him. "Hanging out at the town fair being sociable is the way to get to know people."

"That's what I meant." Gabriel noticed there were only five people in front of him now. His heart rate sped up. Should he kiss a woman his father had such a close relationship with? Clearly Pop had depended upon

Laura for the sense of family he was lacking. It almost felt like Laura could be a sister.

He heard cheers as Buck laid a smooch on Laura. To Gabriel's relief, it was mercifully short and definitely respectful. *Just good clean fun.*

He found himself standing in front of her booth, staring down at her like a nervous schoolboy. Her blue eyes lit on him with curiosity and nothing else, no lingering resentment over their initial meeting. He noted a distressing jump in his jeans, a problem he hadn't anticipated. But he'd always been a sucker for full lips and fine cheekbones. He could smell a sweet perfume, something like flowers in summer.

Laura was nothing like a sister to him.

He laid a twenty-dollar bill on the booth ledge and walked away.

GABRIEL FOUND A BETTER way to support the local elementary school: drinking keg beer some thoughtful and enterprising young man had set up far away from the kissing booth. Here he was safe. No one bothered him while he sat on a hay bale and people-watched, which was good because he really needed to think. He hadn't expected his father to have a family connection in Union Junction.

He sat up. Surely his father hadn't been trying to build his own family here? With a ready-made mom and grandchildren? All it would take was one out of the four brothers to meet the lady and her children, to whom some of the Morgan money had been put in trust, and maybe, just maybe, Pop might get that family he'd been itching for?

He wouldn't put it past Pop. Throw in a scheme that required all four brothers to be on the premises for a year, and Pop had a one in four chance of seeing that dream come true.

Gabriel resolved not to fall for it. In fact, he congratulated himself for staying one step ahead of the wily old man. He didn't know for sure that was what Pop had been up to, but with Pop there was always an angle.

He'd be very cautious.

"Hi." Someone soft and warm slid onto the hay bale beside him. Laura didn't smile at him, but her lips were full and plump from being kissed. "Guess you changed your mind about kissing me."

He hung between fear and self-loathing for being a coward. "Seems we should keep our relationship professional."

"Awkward."

"That, too."

"Fine by me."

He slid her a glance. She had nice breasts under her blue-flowered dress—very feminine. A breast man by nature, he was shocked he hadn't taken note of her physical charms before. He'd been completely preoccupied by the swarm of women descending upon him. Although he had to admit that after just thirty minutes of being in his house, it looked and smelled more welcoming than it was ever going to be under his watch. But now he was checking out Laura's attributes, a subconscious flick of his gaze that dismayed him. God, they really were gorgeous. And he hadn't noticed her small, graceful hands before, either.

He felt his temperature rise uncomfortably. "Where are the kids?" Not that he was really interested, but it was best to remind himself that this woman was a mother, not someone to be ogled as if she were single and available for some casual fun.

Which was all he was interested in, for now and for always. *Damn Pop for throwing temptation my way.*

"Penny and Perrin are being held by some ladies from the church. They're spoiled rotten by them." She pointed to an outdoor play area that had been set up. Lots of older ladies were inside, holding infants and playing games with toddlers.

He could see Penny's light hair, just like her mother's, as she sat in a woman's lap and colored in a book. It wasn't difficult to see what had drawn Pop to this gentle fatherless trio.

Who would have thought Pop would have had a protective bone in his body?

"You know, we're not swindlers. Nor did we lure your father into feeling like we were his family."

He turned to Laura. "I shouldn't have implied that there was anything unusual about my father leaving someone outside the family money. I apologize for that."

"Thank you." She raised her chin. "I knew you could be a difficult person. I choose to ignore that for your father's sake."

He frowned. "I don't want anything for my father's sake."

She shrugged. "He was a nice old man."

"You didn't know him."

"Maybe not as well as you. But maybe better in some ways."

He couldn't argue that. Didn't even want to. "Why?"

"When my husband got sick with cancer, and then died, your father said the least he could do was make certain my kids had college educations. There was a fundraiser here in town to help us...because Dave had no insurance. He was a self-employed carpenter, a dreamer, really." Her voice got soft remembering. "He loved to build homes. The bigger, the better, the more intricate, the better. He did lots of work on your father's place."

This was all beginning to make sense. "Listen, none of this is my business. What my father wants to do with his time and his life is his concern."

She nodded. "I've got to go back to the booth. I've got one more half-hour shift."

He could see the line queuing from here; could count at least twenty men waiting their turn. It looked as if Union Junction had no lack of horny males. "Do you have to kiss all of them?"

"Most of them just kiss my cheek." She smiled. "Only the younger ones try for something more, and a few of the bachelors."

That's what he was afraid of. He thought about his father, and what a jackass he was. He looked at the line, and the men grinning back toward Laura, obviously impatient for her break to be over.

Out of the corner of his eye, he could see Penny, who'd spotted her mother. Mom and daughter waved at each other, and he could see the longing in Laura's eyes to be with her daughter.

What the hell. He lived to be a jackass. He was just keeping the family name alive.

"All right," he announced loudly, ambling to the front of the line, "I'm buying out Ms. Adams's thirty minutes of time." He placed five one hundred-dollar bills—all he had on him at the moment besides some stray ones and a couple of twenties—on the booth ledge where everyone could see his money. Grumbling erupted, but also some applause for the donation. He grunted. "Move along, fellows. The booth is closed for this lady."

Chapter Three

Gabriel's buyout of Laura's time in the kissing booth won him lots of winks from the guys and smiles from the ladies as he walked toward his truck. He hadn't said anything to a shocked Laura—just figured he'd introduced himself to the town in the most obvious way he could have for a man who preferred being a loner.

He didn't even know why he'd done it.

Maybe it was Pop, egging him on to be a gentleman, which was a real stinker of a reason. Mason met him at his truck.

"Have a good time?"

Gabriel checked Mason's eyes for laughter but the question seemed sincere. "Seems like everyone is enjoying themselves."

"Good to see you around. We've been wondering what you're going to do with yourself out there if you stay holed up at the ranch."

"I imagine I'll figure out something."

Mason handed him an envelope. "Mimi said to give you this."

"Mimi?" Gabriel scanned the envelope. It had his name written in his father's handwriting, and no postmark.

"Mimi's the law around here." Mason winked at him.

"What does that have to do with me?"

"Your father left that with her. She asked me to deliver it to you. I've been meaning to get out to your place, but here you are, getting to know the good folks of Union Junction."

Again Gabriel studied him for sarcasm. There appeared to be nothing more to the man's intentions than good old friendliness.

"Why didn't Pop just mail this to me? Or courier it like he did before?"

Mason shrugged. "He said something to Mimi along the lines of when and if any of his sons ever got here, they were to have that. Josiah figured you'd be the first, though. In fact, we wagered on it. I owe your father a twenty." He handed Gabriel a twenty-dollar bill.

Gabriel shook his head. "Put it toward the school fund." He looked at the envelope, wondering why his father would have wagered he'd be the first brother to the ranch. "Who'd you bet on?"

Mason laughed. "Jack. He's the unpredictable one. I always go with the dark horse."

"Cost you this time, buddy."

Mason slapped him on the back. "Sure did. Come on out to the Double M when you have time. We'll introduce you to the kids."

"Maybe I will," Gabriel said, knowing he probably wouldn't.

"Congratulations, by the way," Mason said as he walked away.

"For what?"

"For spending that much money for a kiss and then not getting it. Nerves of steel." Mason waved goodbye. Gabriel glanced back down at the envelope, aware that Mason was now giving him a gentle ribbing. "Jackass," he muttered under his breath and got into his truck.

But it was kind of funny coming from Mason, and even Gabriel had to wonder why he'd passed up the chance to kiss Laura after he'd so obviously put his mark on her.

Not that he was going to think about it too hard.

"NOTHING," LAURA TOLD the girls at the Union Junction Beauty Salon. "I'm telling you, there's nothing between us. He didn't kiss me. Gabriel's barely civil to me."

The girls oohed and then giggled. Laura had received a fair bit of teasing and she expected the kissing booth incident had been thoroughly dissected. Privately, Laura wondered what it would have been like to have Gabriel's lips on hers. It had been so long since she'd kissed a man—well, kissed a man as she had Dave. She didn't count those chaste, predictable pecks in the kissing booth. Even the old ladies and the elderly librarian got their turn in the kissing booth, and the men lined up for them just as quickly. The older ladies—particularly teachers—received grandmotherly busses on the cheek from favorite students.

Everyone was anxious to see the elementary school succeed. There was so much goodwill in this town.

Laura was never going to regret moving here with Dave those five years ago. He'd said Union Junction was a growing town, he'd have lots of work, they'd make a family and be happy out away from the big city....

It had worked out just that way for just over five years. Five perfect years.

So she shouldn't really be thinking about what it would have felt like to kiss Gabriel. She was twenty-six, too old for dreamy longings; she was a mom and a widow.

"I bet he kisses great," one of the stylists said to another, and Laura blushed.

"Aren't you curious?" someone asked her.

Laura ran her hand through Penny's hair as she often did. The feel of the corn-silk softness comforted her, as did the powdery smell of Perrin. "No," she murmured, easy with the lie. "Gabriel is not my kind of man."

They all fell quiet, silenced by the uncomfortable position they had put her in.

"She doesn't need to tiptoe around Dave forever," someone finally spoke up bravely. "Honey, we know you loved him, but you're alive and he wouldn't want you being sad forever."

Tears jumped into Laura's eyes. Several ladies came over to hug her. She felt Penny press closer to her leg. "I know."

"All right, then." They all patted her, then went back to their places. "So next time you get a chance to kiss a hunk like Gabriel Morgan, you just grin and bear it if you want to, okay?"

"Maybe," Laura said, smiling as she wiped away the unwanted tears.

"Wish he'd buy out *my* booth," someone said, and everyone laughed, even Laura, although she really didn't think it was funny. What they didn't realize is that Gabriel hadn't wanted to kiss her, hadn't even looked tempted. He'd sort of picked up his father's responsibility—and then he'd headed off.

A woman knew when a man was interested in her. All fairy tales included a kiss—a man knew how to get what he wanted, even in books. Dave had been a gentle pursuer, slow and careful as if she were a fine porcelain doll.

Gabriel owned no such gentle genes. If he wanted a woman, she figured the indication of his desire would be swift, like a roiling wave breaking over a boat at sea, claiming it with powerful intent.

Gabriel pretty much turned to stone every time he laid eyes on her.

Dear Gabriel,

By now you are at the house and are beginning a year of time you no doubt resent like hell. But money talks and though it might not talk very loud to you, I know you'll stick out the year just to prove yourself. This need of yours to be a tough guy living on the edge is exactly what I now need to lean on.

Remember when I bought that extra acreage and added on to my own hacienda out here? I bought it from a man who was down on his luck, and partly down on his luck thanks to me, which he has discovered. Now don't go getting all high and mighty like I cheated this man out of his birth-

right, because the man is a scoundrel. And anyway, he needed the money.

The problem is, I bought the land suspecting there was an underground oil source. I had it surveyed without his knowledge. He has since found out I paid for a geological survey of his property and feels cheated.

Fact is, maybe he was and maybe he wasn't. He could have paid for his own damn survey.

The trouble in this is that the man is Laura Adams's father, with whom she has no contact due to the fact that he didn't approve of her marrying a carpenter. Didn't like her husband, felt he wasn't good enough for his only child, which didn't set well with Laura. He needed her to marry big to save his sorry ass.

You see my predicament. I could sell the man back his land but the price would include a terrific profit which he cannot afford. I gave Laura's children a tiny portion of what is rightfully theirs, since it would have been anyhow, I suppose, though I believe her father would have drunk up the estate. You might say I just hijacked Penny's and Perrin's inheritance, robbing from the poor to give to the poorer.

Unfortunately, the jackanapes took to threatening me. He really feels cheated by life, and I suppose he has been, but the big dog runs off the little dog and that's life, isn't it? But for the grace of God go I.

Anyway, you'll be seeing him as he lives to

create trouble. But I have faith that you'll smooth
everything over in due time, as you were always
the responsible one in the family, even though it
really chaps your ass that I say that. It just
happens to be true.
　　Pop

"IT DOES CHAP MY ASS." Gabriel forced himself not to
shred his father's letter. "It does indeed chap me like
you can't even imagine, Pop."

He did not appreciate being appointed the protector
of the family fortunes, but even less so the knight of
Laura Adams's little brood. He couldn't even make
himself kiss her; how the hell was he going to start
thinking of her as part and parcel of the Morgan family?

And yet, according to Pop, they owed her something.

What exactly that was, Gabriel wasn't certain.

THE STORM THAT SWEPT Union Junction and the outlying
countryside that night kept Gabriel inside and feeling
caged. He paced the house, watching lightning crack
through the windows of the two-story house. The TV had
gone out; the phone lines were dead. He could hear
water dripping frenzied and fast into the overgrown
gardens.

There wasn't a lot to do in a house one didn't call
home. So far he'd mainly confined himself to his room
on the second floor, and the den. He passed through the
kitchen occasionally to forage from the goodies the
ladies had left for him. The house, he estimated, was

around six thousand square feet. Eventually, he'd have to investigate the rest of Pop's place.

Actually, there was no better time than the present, he decided. The sound of something not quite right caught his ear; instantly he listened intently, all the old survival skills surging into action. Someone was at the front door; someone with a key that wouldn't fit easily. Gabriel considered flinging the door open and confronting whoever was out there, some idiot so dumb they didn't know it was storming like hell outside, then relented. Let the water drown them. If they made it inside, then he'd deal with them.

He thought about Laura's father's threats against Pop and figured he couldn't kill the man in cold blood. So he selected one of his father's many travel guides he had in the den—the heaviest one, something about the South Seas—and waited behind the door.

It suddenly blew open with a gust of wind and rain and vituperative cursing. Gabriel raised the eight-hundred-page tourist guide high over his head, preparing to crack it over his visitor's skull.

"Damn it, I *hate* Texas with a passion!" he heard, and lowered his arms.

"Dane?"

His brother swung to look at him. "What the hell are you hiding back there for? And with a book on the South Seas?"

"Preparing to coldcock you." Gabriel closed the door.

"I'm *supposed* to be here." Dane glared at him, his coat dripping water all over the floor.

"Your e-mail said you were coming in January."

"And I've since changed my mind. You got a problem with that?" Dane asked as he threw his bags in a corner.

Gabriel sighed. "Calm down, Sam Houston. Food's in the fridge."

"Don't call me that. I detest Texas."

In the kitchen, Gabriel settled into a chair. "Are you starting your year of duty early?"

"Figured I might as well get it over with." Dane stuck his head inside the refrigerator door, ending the conversation for the moment. "Fried chicken! Watermelon!"

Gabriel shook his head and began to read the travel guide to the South Seas, which was starting to sound appealing.

"You get your letter from Pop?" Dane asked while he emptied the contents of the fridge on to the kitchen counter.

"What letter?"

"The one with the sob story about watching over this woman and her twins who have no man in the house."

"Twins?" Gabriel sat up. Laura only had a toddler and a baby—didn't she?

"I despise kids almost as much as I hate Texas," Dane said.

Gabriel couldn't think for the shock of adding more kids to Laura's equation. "You're a Texas Ranger. Get over it."

"I'm done. I retired from active duty."

"Congratulations. So back to the family of four—"

"Yeah. I'm supposed to look out for this little mom because of some mess Pop made."

Gabriel frowned. *He* was supposed to be the reluctant knight in shining armor. Possessive emotions and a sense of *I saw her first* crowded his skull.

Dane shuddered. "Her name is Suzy something."

"Suzy? Not Laura?"

Dane sat down across from him with a beer and a plate of fried chicken. "How do you get Laura from Suzy?"

Gabriel shook his head. "This doesn't sound good."

"Tell me about it. I nearly took off for New York, never to be seen or heard from again. But in the end, I knew I had to do this, or I'd really never be free of Pop. He'll try to rule us from the grave if we don't prove to him that nothing he does can screw up our lives anymore."

"And then there's the million bucks."

"A small price for putting up with Pop," Dane said glumly. "You know it's going to get ugly. *Suzy.*" He shuddered.

At least it wasn't Laura Pop had sent Dane to rescue. It didn't really matter, Gabriel reminded himself. One year and he was gone. *Outta here.*

But now apparently there was a family of four in the mix, and an additional *problem* to be solved. Gabriel stared out the window at the pelting rain.

It was indeed beginning to get ugly.

Chapter Four

"So who's Laura, anyway? Girlfriend?"

Gabriel stared at his elder brother, elder being twenty-eight to his own twenty-six. "Hell, no. I just met her. Pop left her children a trust. It's complicated."

"Isn't everything Pop touches complicated?"

Gabriel nodded. "This as much as anything. So what's the deal with Suzy?"

"Don't really know. The letter just said that he owed her something and he'd like me to see to it."

"Pop's matchmaking by making disasters for us to fix."

Dane quit chewing. "You think?"

"Sure. He wants grandkids. He's been busy finding himself some ready-made families."

"Man," Dane said, "that's not fair. I'm glad you figured that out because I might've stepped right into the snare."

Gabriel nodded. "Pop never does anything without a reason."

"But still…family-making?" Dane shook his head. "That's so underhanded."

Gabriel returned to staring out the window.

"So is Laura at least somewhat easy on the eyes?"

Gabriel shrugged. "She is. But she's not my type."

"That would be pretty hard to identify."

He frowned. "What's that supposed to mean?"

Dane looked at him. "Pop's not a sphinx. He can choose all he wants for us, but he can't figure out who'd be that special girl, which personally, I believe is a fairy tale spun to young boys by parents who want grandkids. So we're safe."

"Oh." Gabriel relaxed a little now that he understood his brother wasn't saying he was tough to please. Then he tensed all over again. Pop *had* selected someone Gabriel was attracted to, in a breath-stealing, jaw-tightening way he hadn't anticipated. "I'd still be careful," he warned. "Suzy might be just your thing."

"Nah." Dane shuddered. "I could never hear myself saying 'Suzy, make me breakfast, baby.'"

Gabriel stared at his brother. "You wouldn't say that to a woman without getting a frying pan upside the head."

Dane sipped his beer. "I like girls who can cook."

Gabriel considered that. If the chicken and rice and peas were any forewarning, Laura could definitely cook.

"Great cooking, great sex. Very important qualities in a woman, if I was looking for one. I'd say Pop's run into a brick wall with me. Now you might not be as safe."

Gabriel stood. "I'm going to bed. Make yourself at home, such as it is." He wasn't going to think about sex and Laura; he wasn't going to even kiss her. Or imagine what she tasted like.

"You realize if Pop cooked up a mess for me and one for you, the other two probably have assigned families as well," Dane pointed out.

"Yeah, well, good luck with Jack. We haven't seen him in ten years. And Pete, almost as long." He shrugged. "What's a secret agent going to do with a family?"

"I see Jack's scores every once in a while. He posts a few wins, breaks a few bones. Got stomped in Amarillo."

Gabriel looked at his brother. "Stomped?"

"Not bad. Slight concussion."

He sat again in spite of himself. "You've seen Jack."

"I was a Ranger. I have connections. People tell me things, let me know what's happening on the rodeo circuit." Dane finished the chicken and started on some watermelon. "Sure. When he got stomped, I checked in on him at the hospital. Don't think he knew I was there. He was out of it for a while, but I did see him pat the nurse's ass. And he didn't get his hand slapped."

"I didn't know about Jack being in the hospital."

"You weren't stateside much."

That was true. But even if he had been home, he wouldn't have known much anyway. "So since you hear things, fill me in on Pete."

"He slipped into my house in Watauga about a year ago. I thought I was going to have cardiac arrest when he sat down at my breakfast table with me. I hate that spy crap secret agent voodoo thing he's got going on."

Gabriel grunted. "Thought Rangers had sonar hearing and X-ray vision."

Dane laughed. "We're not quite superhuman, jar-head."

He wasn't a jarhead anymore. Since he'd gotten his discharge, his dark hair had grown out some. He'd expected a bit of gray, and saw a few strands mixed in. No bald spot or thinning hair, though, which made him think he might just keep growing the stuff. It felt strange long. Old habits died hard. "So what did Pete have on his mind?"

"Just checking in. He·was on his way somewhere. Didn't say. Said he was getting tired."

They were all getting older. Even Gabriel felt the gradual march of time slowing his body down, his need for action yet speeding up. Not military action. Something else he hadn't quite put his finger on.

"I don't know if I can live out here for a year," Dane said. "Watauga seemed like hell to me, but this would be worse."

Gabriel took Dane's plate to the sink. "Do any of us really have a choice?" He walked back to the fridge and tossed Dane a beer. "Look. We have to do this. For the sake of our own futures. Pop's crazy, no doubt, but crazy like a fox. Remember? He was always working a deal."

Dane cracked his beer and focused on the label. "I know you're right but it still stinks. I resent Pop for controlling our lives with a snap of his thin fingers."

"Look," Gabriel said, "what if the old man died?" He looked at Dane with a serious expression. "He'd get the last laugh, man. We'd be holding the whole damn bag of emotional dirt."

Dane shook his head. "That's too 'tortured soul' for me."

"Well, think it over because it's true." He sighed and leaned back in his chair, not wanting the conversation, not really wanting the beer, not wanting anything but a flight to Tokyo, maybe. Away from here. "So we're going to do this. And what about Suzy?"

"Now that isn't anything I have to deal with. Whatever mess Pop made, I just have to make certain some money changes hands, some responsibilities are seen to and that's it. I live here for a year, a paltry three hundred and sixty-five days, and then my time is done."

He thought about Laura. "So cut-and-dried."

"So cut-and-dried." Dane nodded. "You got that right."

"Good game plan. I'm turning in."

Gabriel rose, poured the beer into the sink and headed upstairs, mulling over Dane's game plan. It was fairly detached, and Gabriel liked detached and unemotional.

It just might work for him.

LAURA FROWNED AT THE NOTE that had been stuck to the front door of her small house. *Hey, baby, be by to see you later.*

Chills ran through her. Nobody *baby'd* her—no one except her father. She didn't want to see him. Didn't want him near her children. The fact that he'd found out where she lived made her want to move far away, as fast as she could.

He was her father by blood, but Mr. Morgan had acted more fatherly toward her. There was something wrong with the man whose genes she bore—Ben had problems with thinking the world owed him something.

A chip on his shoulder kept him from being the responsible human he might have been.

Laura wanted no part of him.

She took her children inside and locked the door. Penny went straight to her stuffed animals, so Laura put Perrin in his playpen before she sank into a chair at the kitchen table to think.

There was a reason Ben had chosen this moment to filter back into her life. Months ago, Ben had claimed Mr. Morgan had done him a disservice, which the old man had denied. Ben had told her that Mr. Morgan had cheated him out of money. She didn't think Mr. Morgan was the cheating type but after Dave died, he had put that money into trust for her kids. Was it guilt money? At the time, tired and grief-stricken, she'd assumed it was exactly what he'd said it was, a gift of college education for kids whose company he'd enjoyed. As a teacher, she'd certainly appreciated the gesture. A lot of people had been very generous after the funeral. In fact, the Jeffersons had helped pay down the mortgage on this house so that Laura wouldn't have to struggle so much. It was just the type of caring thing Laura had seen done many times over in this town.

She hadn't thought about guilt money. And Ben had always been the kind of man who whined. It was part of the reason she was determined to shoulder her burdens without complaining, without relying on other people. She wanted independence and that didn't come by whining and blaming.

She thought about Gabriel. He seemed very independent, too. He wouldn't blame other people for any misery he incurred. She'd heard from Mr. Morgan that none of their family was close, a fact that disheartened him. In his twilight years—he'd started to say he was feeling his age—he had hoped to knit his family back together.

He'd never said exactly what the problem had been.

Laura wanted a family for her children, though. If she ever remarried, she would want a man who was close to his kin. Penny and Perrin deserved a father who didn't have skeletons rattling in his closet; they had enough bones with Ben. Although they'd never met him, it was only a matter of time before that family skeleton made a nuisance of itself with some whiny rattling.

She tore up the note and threw it into the trash, pushing it down deep before closing the shutters and checking the locks on the doors.

Two hours later, Laura had the kids in bed. She'd been spending some time making plans for the upcoming school year; it would be her second year teaching seventh-grade science. Laura had plans for setting up some conservation composts and doing a rocket launch. If the students were ready, she planned to jump right into some in-class science projects that they could record data over the course of the whole year.

She'd completely put Ben out of her mind.

Someone knocked at the door, and the dreaded prickles ran up her back. She closed her eyes, reminding herself that Ben was her father, that he had never been violent. He just hadn't liked Dave and had been disagreeable and opinionated about him.

It was Mr. Morgan he'd really been at odds with. Maybe she'd been influenced by those stories.

Yet there was the money. Funny that Ben would be showing up in her life when he knew that her children had been the recipients of various gifts of goodwill from the town. Ben wasn't a coincidental kind of man; he planned everything almost down to an obsession. Then again, she'd heard through the grapevine that Ben had picked up heavy drinking in the town that bordered Union Junction.

The knock sounded again. Now was as good a time as any to face her father. Then again, it could be Mimi.

Mimi would call first.

"Who is it?"

"Gabriel Morgan."

She put a hand to her chest to still her thundering heart, then realized he made her just as nervous—in an unexpected, different way.

She turned on the porch light and opened the door. "Hello."

There he was, wearing a Western hat and jeans. He wasn't smiling, but he hadn't smiled the other times she'd met him, either. He had bought out her kissing booth—and then disappeared. She'd expected to hear something from him…she hadn't been sure what.

"I would have called, but I didn't have your number. Guess it's unlisted."

She nodded. "It is."

"Would have called Mason for it, but…hope you don't mind me stopping by."

He seemed uncomfortable and Laura didn't blame him. Apparently he was only in the area because of his duty to his father. She held the door open so Gabriel could come inside. "If you'd called Mason, he would have asked why you needed to see me. I can ask you myself." Laura pointed to a sofa so he could sit down. He did, gingerly hovering on the flowered sofa.

"Just seems we got off on the wrong foot."

She nodded. "Maybe. What other foot is there, though?"

He hesitated. "I think I was surprised my father left me instructions about you."

"He did?" That wasn't welcome news. She didn't want Gabriel to feel obligated to her in any way.

"Yeah. Apparently you have some issues with your father, who may or may not have your best interests at heart."

She thought about the note on the door. "It's not something I really want to talk about."

"I fully understand. I don't want to talk about my dad, either."

"So don't." She felt more awkward by the second. "Look, Gabriel, despite whatever your father told you, I can take care of myself. I have lots of friends. I have a great job. I love my kids. I don't need a protector or anything like that."

He glanced down at his hands for a moment before looking back at her. "You're sure you're all right?"

"Of course I am! Your father was ultraprotective of me because of my children. But you don't have to take on a parenting role, Gabriel. I wouldn't want you to.

They had a father." She took a deep breath. "He was a wonderful man, and…I'm not looking to fill his role in our lives."

He appeared to consider her words. "You'd let me know if you need something?"

"Honestly, no." She shook her head. "I wouldn't. I'd call Mimi or some of my girlfriends. But I can tell you I would if that's the closure you need. It just won't be true. You're completely off the hook."

A knock at the door startled both of them. A shaky premonition snapped into Laura.

"I'm sorry. I didn't realize you were expecting company." Gabriel got to his feet.

"Laura! Baby! Let me in!"

Gabriel frowned. Laura glanced at the door, making certain it was securely locked after she'd let Gabriel in. To her relief, it was.

"Laura! It's your father. Don't keep me out here!"

"I didn't realize you were still on speaking terms with Ben." Gabriel's eyes searched hers. "Thought I'd heard the opposite."

It was her family's private business. "I don't want to discuss this with you." If she did, he would feel responsible for her.

The glass pane smashed, and Laura screamed in spite of herself. She flung open the door. "Ben, what the hell? You could have hurt one of the children!"

"Hi, baby." Her father tipped unsteadily to one side, listing, before righting himself. "I know I taught you better manners than to leave your old dad standing outside."

She felt Gabriel move behind her. She pushed him back with one hand. This was her problem. "Ben, take your drunk and sorry self off my property and don't come back. We said all we had to say years ago. If you ever come around here again, or if I catch you near my children, I'm going to have you put in jail."

He squinted at her. "Who's that in there with you?"

"Ben, pay attention to what I'm saying to you—" Laura began, but her father shoved the door back so fast she couldn't stop him.

"Morgan," her father said, his tone a curse. "I should have known Morgan's pups wouldn't be far away from the prize."

Gabriel literally moved her from the door, filling the opening with his large frame. "Ben, whatever happened between you and my dad is old news. It has no part with me, and it has no part with Laura. You need to let it go."

"The money your father gets from the oil rights on that property should be mine."

"So take it to court," Gabriel said calmly. "You can't get any money that Laura has because it's all tied up in trust for her children."

"That's why you're hanging around. The children." Ben's face grew surly. "Like little pieces of gold."

"I'd be a fairly useless human if I had to wait around for fifteen years to get some little kid's trust. Move along, Ben. It's all over. Laura said she didn't want you here, and you need to respect that."

"Because you say so?"

Laura tried to edge in front of Gabriel but he held her back.

"Because I say so," Gabriel confirmed. "I'd be going if I was you, or you're not going to be in one piece to do it on your own."

Ben's face wrinkled with hate. "You haven't heard the last of me, Morgan."

"I'm certain of that." Gabriel shut the door, waiting until he heard Ben's boots leave the porch before he turned to Laura. "I'll fix this pane before I go. I can tape it tonight, and then get some glass tomorrow at the hardware shop."

She straightened her five-foot-two frame. "Don't ever fight my battles for me again. Don't assume I can't take care of myself."

"It wasn't about you," Gabriel said, "it was about my father and his schemes." He glanced around the room. "I'll be sleeping here tonight."

Chapter Five

Gabriel's pronouncement clearly didn't suit Laura, but he hadn't expected it would. She gave him a determined stare. "You will not be sleeping here tonight, or any other time."

"Mommy?"

Gabriel turned to face a tiny blue-eyed, blond version of her mother. Penny stood in the hallway, rubbing sleepy eyes.

"Yes, honey?" Laura said, going to her.

"I heard a loud noise."

Laura shot Gabriel a warning glance. "A pane on the door accidentally broke. Don't worry about a thing."

In the background, Perrin began to cry. Gabriel focused on the sound. If he had to guess—and he had zero experience with infants—it was a *comfort me* cry.

Laura went down the hall to Perrin. Penny looked solemnly at Gabriel. "Who's going to fix the window?"

"I am," he told her. "Tomorrow morning."

"No, you're not," Laura said, entering the family room with Perrin, who was happy now that he was being held. "And you're definitely not—" she glanced at Penny "—you're definitely not staying here," she said in a low voice.

"Either I stay here or your family comes to my ranch. You can't stay here with your father in a hotheaded state." Protective emotions inside him rushed to the surface. Laura looked vulnerable with her two children in her arms. She was trying to be tough but her eyes held confusion. He knew she had to be scared. No woman wanted to sleep in a house with a broken window. If Ben came back—and he probably was watching to see when Gabriel's truck left—he'd simply reach through that pane and unlock the door.

To Gabriel's mind, any battle Ben wanted to put up should be with Gabriel, not Laura. He was after money, pure and simple. The easiest way to get it was to panhandle his own daughter.

"I'm going to put my children back to bed."

Laura turned and went down the hall. Penny followed with a backward glance at Morgan, her face somber. His heart lurched, twisted. Despite his vow to never want children of his own, Penny's big eyes and soft voice saying his name stole his heart. Perrin's plump cheeks and soft hair made him want to see the little boy have his chance at growing up safe and strong. Actually, he would have loved to hold the baby if Laura would let him—but he knew she would not. She had definitely warned him off her deceased husband's territory. He couldn't blame her for that. But she did need some help, whether she wanted to admit it or not.

Maybe Pop hadn't been so crazy after all.

Laura walked into the kitchen with Penny, getting the little girl a drink of water. She held her daughter in her lap, singing softly to her, ignoring Gabriel. That was fine with him. Frankly, he'd never seen anything so beautiful as Laura comforting her daughter.

Then he heard Perrin crying again, an inconsolable sobbing. Gabriel started to mention to Laura that the baby was upset again, then thought better of it. Penny was enjoying her mother's attention. Gabriel quietly went down the hall in the direction of the crying—three bedrooms, bathroom on the hall to the left—and found the nursery.

Perrin had wedged himself under his tiny pillow and flailed a blanket over himself, and was not happy about his predicament.

"Hey, little guy." Gabriel removed the blanket. The baby stared up at him. "Don't be so upset, dude. Your mom's trying to calm your sister down, and they just need a moment together. You've got this soft bed, and everything's going good for you, right? So calm down." He reached into the crib, stroking the baby's cheek. Perrin watched him with big eyes. Gabriel couldn't stand it any longer. Laura would not appreciate this, but the lure was too strong.

He scooped the baby up and cradled him to his chest.

There was nothing, he decided, quite like the smell of a baby. The feel of a baby. And this one…this one was so rotund and squeezable… Gabriel closed his eyes as the baby laid his head against his chest. He felt like he was holding one of those fat cherubim he'd seen in paintings in the Louvre.

The baby had gotten himself agitated with all his wailing. Gabriel swept back Perrin's tiny curls from his forehead. "Little man, you've got to learn to chill. There's nothing quite as annoying as getting yourself wrapped up in your blanket, but you've got to learn to think your way out of your predicament." He leaned his cheek against the baby's head. "When you're older, of course. Right now, you have the luxury of having a good wail on the world. When you're my age, you learn to suck it up." Gently, he placed Perrin back in his crib, and quietly hummed a Texas cowboy lullaby he'd learned long ago. Soothed, the baby curled into his sheet, opened his eyes once more, then shut them peacefully.

Gabriel backed away from the crib, yet kept his eye on the baby, kept humming. That hadn't been so bad.

"What are you doing?"

Gabriel turned. "He was crying."

"I can take care of my own family, Gabriel."

He looked at Laura. "I noticed. Relax. Where's Penny?"

"In bed."

He nodded. "Guess I'll head to the sofa and do the same." Brushing past her, knowing the storm of protest was brewing at his back, he almost smiled. Laura was independent, she was in a bad spot and there was nothing like the combination to make a woman like her mad.

"It's inappropriate for a man to stay in a house with a newly widowed woman and her children. What would my neighbors say?"

"Folks'll understand when they hear about your visitor."

"*I* won't understand!" She had her hands on her hips and was building anger. He gave her credit for stubbornness.

"Suit yourself." He nodded. "I'll be back tomorrow to fix the window."

"I'll call a handyman."

She sure didn't seem to like him. It hurt his feelings a bit since she'd been so fond of his father. Or had she? Had her affection been a ruse for his money?

It didn't matter—all those answers would come in time. "Good night." He headed outside, got in his truck and made himself comfortable.

Ten minutes later, she was at his truck window.

"What are you doing?" she demanded.

He turned down the radio, which was playing soft country tunes. "Watching out for the boogeyman."

"I don't need you to protect me." Laura shook her head. "What's it going to take to get that through your thick skull?"

"Something more than you've got, lady, because I'm not convinced you don't need a little help. And as long as I'm out here, and you're in there, I'd say your virtue is safe."

She gave him a glare that would have curdled milk.

"What's the problem?" he asked reasonably. "I'm not bothering you."

"You're the problem. Go away."

He got out of the truck, considering her. "I'm slowly starting to figure you out."

"You are not."

"Yeah. I am. Here's my offer. I'll stay out here until I'm satisfied you're safe. In the morning, you call the handyman, or Mason, and I'll go." He put his hands on either side of her, capturing her against the truck. "And in the meantime, I'll be a gentleman. I promise."

Then he kissed her.

Gently, but he kissed her all the same.

At the moment, it felt awesome. For days afterward, he'd wish he hadn't.

SHOCKED BY GABRIEL'S KISS, Laura pushed his arms away. She stared at him, trying to figure out why he'd done it—hadn't he just said he'd be a gentleman?— then stalked inside her house, locking the door.

She let out her breath and waited for her thundering heart to still. He was everything Josiah Morgan had said his son was: arrogant, opinionated, stubborn.

Nothing like Dave, who'd been gentle, kind, nurturing.

And she'd been lying when she'd told Gabriel she didn't need him standing guard. She was indeed afraid, mostly for Penny and Perrin. Her father wouldn't hurt her children, but it was nerve-wracking and wearying when Ben was drunk like that.

Yet no woman wanted to be a responsibility. She knew Mr. Morgan's bequest made Gabriel feel he had to have a part in looking after her and her children.

She touched a finger to her lips, still surprised that she remembered the way his kiss had felt.

She was afraid of feeling anything.

It hadn't been long enough since her husband's passing to feel anything. Hadn't she promised to love and honor Dave until the day she died? Her heart would never forget him.

No other man should have a part in her children's lives. Perhaps that's why she'd felt so comfortable with Mr. Morgan's affection for Penny and Perrin; it was grandfatherly and safe. Their own grandfather was rough around the edges; Dave's family lived up north and sent presents at Christmas. Mr. Morgan had provided the love the children needed through Laura's most devastating hours. She would not feel the same about Gabriel sharing their lives.

Yet he was out in her driveway, standing guard over them. She'd frozen when she'd heard him singing to Perrin; very few men would sing to another man's children. She'd found that quiet act of his astonishingly sexy. Tingles sizzled over her skin, jolting her with a memory she'd shared only with her husband.

Yet those emotions were impossible. Ignoring the tug of desire she would never acknowledge, she went to put on her nightgown and go to bed.

"THEN WHAT HAPPENED?" Dane stared at his brother. Hot Texas sun rose to nearly overhead, indicating the noon hour. The steaming humidity was suffocating. "Did you kick Ben's ass?"

"No." Gabriel peered at the cracked rocky earth where the old dividing line had been, before Pop had bought Ben's property. "I sent him on his way and then stayed to make certain he didn't return."

Dane knelt, watching Gabriel dig around in the soil. "So now what? What are we looking for?"

"I don't know. Pop and his wild tale of oil under the land he bought from Ben. I don't believe it should be causing this much trouble, because if there was enough oil to fight over, Pop would have had drillers out here by now." He looked at Dane. "So what if it was one of Pop's wild tales? What if he was trying to stir Ben up on purpose?"

"Why would he?"

"I just don't trust Pop." He couldn't tell anything about the earth. The soil didn't look any different to him, from the miles he and Dane had walked together. He didn't really need Dane tagging along, but he couldn't say it had been a bother. Pop had claimed he'd noticed a difference in the soil that led him to speculate that the land was holding a secret, but Gabriel was more inclined to believe a fairy tale had been dreamed up for all of them.

"Well, I will be damned," Dane said, and Gabriel glanced up.

"What?"

"Look what the wind just blew into town."

There wasn't so much as a breeze to stir the humidity. Gabriel turned. "Pete," he murmured, shocked. "I'll be damned right along with you."

Their brother rode up on a horse, a chestnut Gabriel recognized as one of their own. "It isn't February."

"Nope." Pete got down. "But thanks for the trail you left for me."

"Trail?" Gabriel stared at his brother, realizing that the years had left them all a little older, a little leaner, maybe a little meaner. Pete's eyes were a hard dark granite; his cheeks sculpted by whatever demons secret agents battled. He was surprised that he was glad to see his brother. "We didn't leave you a trail."

"Tire marks to the side of the field, hay bent after that. Looked like a bear had crossed the field instead of two men."

"We weren't trying to hide where we were," Dane said. "Good to see you, Pete. Didn't know you were in the country."

"You might have thought about hiding if you knew Ben Smith was at the house, hollering about wanting Gabriel to come out and take his punishment."

"Oh, hell." Gabriel winced. "He's becoming a pain."

"I sent him on his way, but he's convinced we owe him money," Pete said. "He shared that at the top of his lungs, over and over again. Do we?"

Gabriel shrugged. "I doubt it." He glanced at the ground. "Think Pop's got everybody all stirred up for nothing."

"You mean this isn't going to be the next King Ranch?" Pete asked, his hard gaze turning lighter for a moment. "Ben seems to think we're sitting on a Spindletop-sized gusher."

"Don't think so." Gabriel turned toward the truck. "Thanks for the warning, though."

Dane followed, and Pete remounted, riding alongside. "We probably want to keep an eye on him."

Something—maybe a fly—whizzed past Gabriel's ear. He flicked at it, then realized the fly had been accompanied by a sound in the distance.

"What the hell was that?" Dane suddenly flattened Gabriel to the ground.

Gabriel heard hoofbeats rhythmically charging away from them. "Did that sorry sack of crap just take a shot at me?"

"Pete's going after him. Lie low until we know Pete's ridden him down."

Hay crackled in Gabriel's face and itched at his hot skin. He wasn't too keen that his brother felt he had to protect him. "Get the hell off of me. I'm not china, and that goofball couldn't hit the broadside of a barn." Gabriel preferred to take his own hit—he didn't need to rely on his brothers. Dane didn't move, and Gabriel couldn't hold back a snarl. "Get *off,* damn it!"

Dane rolled away. Gabriel jumped to his feet, making a primo target of himself in his red T-shirt and jeans.

"I'd get down if I were you until Pete signals. Who's going to look after Mrs. Adams and the children if you're gone?"

Gabriel glared hotly enough at his brother to scorch the hay around him. "Be very careful, brother."

"Oh, hell. You always were the sensitive one." Dane laughed, untroubled by his brother's foul mood.

Gabriel ignored the desire to jump on Dane and whale him a good one. "I suppose you don't think Pete makes a bigger target on the back of a horse."

"Ben's aiming for you, not Pete."

Gabriel grunted. "I'm walking to the truck. If Ben could have hit me, he would have by now."

"It just takes one lucky shot."

He wasn't going to cower on the ground while his brother fought his battle. If he got his hands on Ben, he was going to wring his skinny neck.

Then again, Ben was Laura's father. Theoretically, he shouldn't strangle the ornery little coward. Laura would probably say he'd bullied Ben, and she sure wouldn't want any help solving her own family issues. Something round in the dry grass caught his eye. Gabriel bent to pick it up. "Not that I'm any happier about a BB, but at least I'm not going to have to kill him."

They got in the truck and he and Dane drove back to the house in silence. Dane got out and glanced over his shoulder. "Coming in?"

He shook his head. "Got to get some glass for Laura's window in town."

Dane studied him for a long moment, then nodded. "I'll see what Pete found."

Gabriel didn't really care. All he was thinking about was Laura and the kids.

LAURA KNEW GABRIEL WAS out there. She knew when he drove into the driveway. She didn't answer the door when he rang the bell. Holding her breath, she waited for him to leave, knowing she was being unkind, maybe even rude, by not thanking him for his care of her.

She didn't want big, strong Gabriel Morgan pushing his way into her life, storming her heart. It could happen so easily. But she was going to fight the onslaught of his charisma with all her might, for the sake of her own sanity.

Would she even breathe until she heard his truck drive away? She didn't think so; her chest physically pained her. He rang the bell again, calling, "Laura! Your door needs to be repaired!"

He wasn't leaving until he did what he'd come to do. She opened the door silently, unsmiling. He tipped his cowboy hat to her, then puttied in the window efficiently and quietly, never meeting her gaze.

When he finished, he closed the door and went whistling down the porch. Now that he was gone, she could relax. Her house was safe again.

Except it wasn't. There might not be a broken window anymore, but there was a very strong chance of a broken heart that had too few pieces left to risk shattering.

She locked the door.

LAURA THOUGHT SHE WAS free until she heard Gabriel's truck pull back into her drive at eight o'clock that night. She tensed, waiting for a knock on the door, but none came. Burning curiosity tweaked at her. She peeked out the window. He'd simply shut off the engine and pulled out a newspaper.

An hour later she couldn't ignore him any longer. She went outside to confront him. "This is not necessary."

"Caution is a good thing. Besides, your old man took a shot at me this morning."

She gasped, not wanting to believe him. The honest depth of his eyes made her realize he was being completely truthful. She felt sick over her father's spiral into violence. "Did you call the sheriff?"

He shook his head. "Nah. It was only a BB. Pete ran your father down and Ben said he'd just been shooting at a duck. I didn't see any ducks, but whatever." He looked at her with some sympathy. "Maybe there's a way you know of that we can calm him down, get him to stop acting like he's out of his tree."

"I appreciate you trying to be understanding, but I don't know what Ben's problem is. We haven't been close since the day I got married." Instinctively, she lifted her chin. It was still a memory that hurt. "I'm not sure why he'd want to hurt you, though."

"He was just trying to get attention." Gabriel shrugged. "Pete paid him some."

"Pete? How many of you are at the ranch now?"

"Three."

She smiled. "That leaves just one more. Guess your father knew what he was doing."

That rankled. "Go on in before the kids start looking for you. I'm going to read the newspaper."

She sighed, wearing a slightly annoyed expression. "I have a phone. I'll call you if Ben comes back. How's that? You go on home and visit with your brothers, the way your father intended."

He squinted at her. "How do you know what my dad intended?"

She shrugged. "Josiah wasn't exactly quiet about how much he missed his sons being around."

That seemed strange. He'd pretty much run them off when they were old enough to be gone.

"Do you think your father really stole from my father the way Ben claims?"

Gabriel considered that. "I don't know what to believe. And I'm not sure it really matters."

"It matters to Ben."

"Are you taking sides?"

She shook her head. "Merely stating a fact."

"Even if my father did steal from him, that doesn't mean he has the right to knock out your window and take a shot at me."

"I didn't say it did. I simply said that he certainly feels wronged."

"Yeah, well." He wished she'd get on another topic that was friendlier to both of them, and a little easier. Getting a laugh or a smile out of Laura was rare. The shame of it was, he liked looking at her so much. He wished she'd stop cornering him all the time so he could just sit and stare at her full lips and blue eyes. Right now she was wearing a white blouse and a blue skirt that looked cool and feminine. He liked the whole modest thing she had going on. "Well, I'd best turn in," he said, before he started hungering for something he couldn't have.

"Turn in?"

"Get some shut-eye." He settled the newspaper over his face. "I've got some chores to take care of early in the morning."

"Nothing is going to happen. You really don't have to stay."

He slid the newspaper off and met her gaze, not to be polite but because he wanted an excuse to look at her. "I know it won't, not as long as I'm sitting in your drive-way."

"You're the most stubborn man I ever met."

"Yes, ma'am."

"Have it your way." She turned away, and without any guilt he watched her fanny sashay to the house and up the steps.

He knew he shouldn't look. A gentleman wouldn't. *Damn.*

Chapter Six

One hour after he'd read the sports section, the business section and the larger community section of Union Junction's newspaper—a one-page epistle—Gabriel was surprised when the passenger-side door of his truck opened and Laura slid into the seat.

"Hello," he said cautiously.

She gave him a determined look. "Why did you kiss me?"

He didn't have an easy answer for that question; he'd pondered it and come up empty. The only reason he could think of was that the old rascal inside him had risen up and acted impulsively. "Paid for it, I guess. Just cashed in a bit late."

She nodded at his reply. "Gabriel, I can't have you sitting in my drive every night. It's only six o'clock now, and here you are already. It's not good for me."

"The neighbors will talk?"

"You and I both know that was just an excuse."

"So what's the real reason you don't want me around?"

She took a deep breath, met his gaze. "I just might fall for you, just like your father probably planned."

His jaw slackened. "Excuse me if I didn't see that one coming."

"Neither did I. But I've been thinking a lot about this, and I realized my heart is just a bit too tender right now. You know, a woman gets lonely. She gets scared at times. And if there's a big, strong man in her driveway, she could just get used to that."

"You're talking in the third person, which means you're not referring to yourself, which means you're likely telling me a story." He frowned at her. "What's the real thing you're trying to tell me?"

She looked at him, silent.

"Correct me if I'm wrong, but you don't strike me as the kind of woman who falls for a man who gives her a light smooch."

Laura sighed. "All right. I am telling you a bit of a story."

"Why?"

"So you'll leave." She shook her head. "I really, really want you to go away."

He was slightly hurt. "All you had to do was ask."

"I have been asking, but you're ignoring me. You'll do whatever you want to, all the time."

"Sorry. Guess I've been on my own all my life."

"Do not try to win pity from me."

He heard her softening and it cheered him. "You didn't have to get my hopes up like that, with all that business about falling for me." Two could play at her game.

She gave him a long stare. "Gabriel, I doubt your hopes were up."

"You never know. I have sensitive feelings."

She looked out the window toward the house, making no comment.

"So you were trying to scare me off with all that business about falling for me. It was just reverse psychology."

She smiled and shook her head. "Obviously it didn't work."

"It did work a little," he said. "I know now that you've been thinking about my kiss. Pretty good for a guy who only got a one-second pass at your lips. Imagine how much more unforgettable I'd be if you'd give me, say, a full hour—"

She got out of the truck and stomped inside. He laughed softly to himself. Maybe she did want him.

If that was the case, he'd probably not say no.

But the children…he was not father material, he knew that. And Laura was not a one-night kind of woman.

Sighing, he turned on his truck, and against his better judgment, acceded to her wishes by leaving her alone. He didn't like it, but she was right: he was too stubborn for his own good.

"Thought you were spending the night out," Dane said, glancing up from the game of chess he and Pete were playing. "It's only six-thirty."

"I was. Sensing that I'm not entirely welcome at the Adams homestead, I decided to come back home and bother you." Gabriel felt restless. He prowled the kitchen looking for something to eat, but he wasn't hungry. Wasn't thirsty. Just had energy to spare.

"She ran you off?" Pete laughed. "To think we used to be such ladies' men, and now we sit here playing checkers."

"Chess," Dane said.

"Whatever. Check."

Dane squinted at the board. "I will be damned. How did you do that?"

Pete leaned back and looked at Gabriel while Dane pondered his next move. "Now what?"

"She thinks we're all square and that we don't owe her anything." Gabriel figured Laura was right. He wouldn't want anybody trying to take care of him, either. He remembered how he'd felt when all the ladies had rushed his house with goodies—he hadn't wanted that at the time. How Laura felt was not that unreasonable.

"Well, while we're all here, we probably ought to discuss what we're going to do about this shack." Pete looked at him. "Don't you think?"

Since Laura didn't need him, it was probably best. She'd really stung him with that drama about how she might fall for him. Part of him had really jumped when she'd started that spiel, and to his surprise, he'd found himself listening eagerly. To find out she'd just been creating a tale to run him off really wounded his pride. "Guess so."

Dane glanced up as the chess clock dinged. He punched the button down. "Your turn. By the way, Gabriel, you realize you're falling into Pop's plot."

"So how's Suzy?" Gabriel asked. "The girl you're supposed to rescue?"

Pete frowned. "Pop didn't send me a letter about anyone. Why'd you guys get one?"

"Be glad." Gabriel sat down. "Or you could have Dane's Suzy."

"Yeah," Dane said. "That'd be awesome."

"So back to this shack of Pop's," Pete said. "We're going to have to hire some people to work it. I'm thinking Ben might be a good first choice."

"Are you out of your mind?" Gabriel demanded.

Pete shrugged. "Best to keep your enemy firmly tucked up against your bosom."

Gabriel blinked, not liking the idea at all. "I don't need Ben around here. He's a lazy drunk."

"Maybe he needs a fair chance." Dane moved a rook on the board and looked satisfied.

"Did you two cook this up while I was at Laura's? I think you're trying to get me killed or something." Gabriel shrugged. "Not that he could get at me. I never knew a man with such bad aim."

Pete nodded. "You'd be safer with him around drawing a paycheck."

"Okay," Gabriel said slowly, "so Ben manages to work one square inch of this ranch. We'll need other hands."

"So are you agreeing?" Dane asked.

"I guess. I can always beat him like a piñata if he acts up."

"No beating the help," Pete said. "That will not win you points with Laura."

"I'll never have points with Laura." As he said it, Gabriel realized it was true, though he hadn't meant to sound so down about it. "We're on different sides of the world, so far apart we'll never run into each other."

His brothers went back to their heated rivalry on the chessboard, the subject closed now that they'd gotten their way about hiring Ben. Gabriel grimaced—what a dumb idea that was. But they were his older brothers, and he'd just get voted down anyway. Life was always hell on the baby.

The notion made him think about Laura and her baby. He wondered if Perrin was suffering from an upset stomach tonight, he wondered if Penny was sleeping soundly tucked in her bed. For that matter, he'd love to know if Laura was sleeping soundly tucked in her bed, then decided that train of thought was fruitless. "Just going to get me in trouble," he murmured, and Pete glanced up.

"What?" his brother asked.

"Nothing," Gabriel said. "See you two troublemakers in the morning."

"Checkmate," Dane said triumphantly, and Gabriel left them arguing over who was the better chess player. They'd both checkmated him, and what he couldn't fathom was why.

TEN YEARS AGO, THEY HAD been out at a rodeo, all four boys. Pop did not approve of sneaking out, and he despised rodeos with a vengeance. He was determined to keep everyone under his roof, and therefore under his thumb. This came under the heading of good parenting.

The boys chafed, resenting their father's strict rules.

Later, they would think he was pretty reasonable, but then, they deployed every tactic possible to get away from him. Gabriel just wanted to be with his older brothers—he was sixteen, and that seemed reasonable. The boys wouldn't have gone if they hadn't believed they were safe. Jack would never have done anything to harm any of them; he was their hero. Since he was the oldest, Jack took his responsibilities seriously, and yet, Pop considered him a drifter with no purpose in life. Jack hung around rodeos, played his guitar at night, loved the girls a little too eagerly.

Pop had told Jack he belonged in the military when he turned eighteen, and that really began the divide between them. Pop wanted his sons' lives to have a purpose. Jack would not be allowed to live the wild lifestyle of rodeo.

Though Jack was supposed to be helping Pop on the ranch, he'd been riding bulls for years. The brothers never told on him. They decided to sneak out one night and watch him in a town two hours away. Jack had drawn a bull named Ace of Death, a bull in the running for being a registered bounty bull. A rider with big dreams and the determination to stick with it, Jack had looked forward to the challenge.

Six seconds and a fractured spine later, the boys had rushed behind the ambulance, following Jack to the hospital. They got T-boned at an intersection, and though it hadn't been their fault and nobody was hurt, all the brothers had been in for Josiah Morgan's anger. He hadn't spared it. He blamed Jack for luring his brothers out, blamed Pete and Dane for allowing Gabriel to go, blamed Gabriel for not telling his father what the older boys were planning.

Pop's anger had been a terrible thing to witness.

Gabriel shook his head, telling himself that going back down memory lane wasn't a good idea. Better to live in the present.

He turned and headed back toward his brothers. "When are you going to offer Ben a job?"

"Offer it yourself. He's sitting on the back porch," Dane said.

"Why?" Gabriel wasn't eager to speak to the cantankerous old man.

"He's lonely," Pete said. "He's been quiet as a mouse."

"I don't want any part of this scheme." Gabriel scratched his head. "I don't think you two know what you're doing. He broke Laura's window, you do remember that?"

Dane shrugged. "We can always fire him, Gabriel. It's just best to keep him here—him and his little cap gun."

They listened, hearing the sound of a car pull into the front yard. "Company," Pete said. He peered out. "Looks like Ben has a caller."

Gabriel frowned. "Who would come here to see him?"

"His daughter. And grandchildren, from the looks of things." Dane eyed the black-and-white pieces on the board. "Couldn't hurt to say hello."

Gabriel peered out the window, watching Laura in a pretty sundress step around the back of the house, her two children in tow. "How does she know where he is?"

"We told her," Dane said. "We, of course, wanted her opinion on how she would feel about us offering her father a job."

"And when was I going to be consulted?" Gabriel began to have misgivings about how wise it was for the three of them to be occupying a house together.

"We thought you were at Laura's," Pete said reasonably as Gabriel resumed spying on Laura talking to her father. "We didn't realize when you said you were going to Laura's that you meant no farther than her driveway."

"That's sort of a metaphor, isn't it?" Dane glanced at him, a sly twinkle in his eyes. "The princess won't let the drawbridge down for fair knight."

Pete snickered. "No Holy Grail for him."

"Very funny." Gabriel watched Laura sit down next to her father, gently introducing him to the children. "It seems rude to make them sit outside and visit."

"Nah. They want some time to themselves. Probably like for you to stop staring like a Peeping Tom through the window. I'm getting a beer. You want one?" Pete asked Dane, ignoring Gabriel.

To his credit, Ben seemed thrilled to see the children. He sat up from his slouched position, touching first Penny's hand, then Perrin's. Laura stood back a pace from her father, cautious, yet seemingly hopeful. "Do you think broken families can forget the past?" Gabriel murmured, thinking about the bad feelings between Laura and her father.

"Jeez," Pete said, "no one ever said we had to love each other or anything. We just have to live together.

It's one year. No longer than being in a college dorm with a bad roommate."

"Or being married to the wrong woman for a year," Dane said. "Anyway, this house is big enough for three families."

"And we could add on to it if things get really grim." Pete glanced at Gabriel. "As long as we're under this one roof, Pop never said how big the roof had to be."

"We're not adding on to anything. I meant if Laura and Ben could put their bad blood behind them, we can, too." Gabriel wished he didn't feel so odd man out all of a sudden. Like everybody in the room had been chosen for football and he was designated water boy. "I just don't get the theory behind hiring Ben."

"Every man needs a purpose." Dane looked at him. "Go ask him. You're the human resources director of this ranch."

Gabriel looked at Laura through the slatted wood blinds. "And how did that become my responsibility?"

"You're the baby. Plus, you have a yen for that woman and her children. Pop must have known you better than you know yourself." Dane leaned back in the leather chair, staring up at the rough-beamed ceiling. "I'd almost be scared about Suzy, but I know myself better than that."

"So when do you find out about the mysterious Suzy?" Gabriel put off going out to talk to Laura and Ben. They seemed calm together, maybe even enjoying each other's company for the first time in God only knew how many years.

"Never." Dane grinned, then high-fived his brother. "Dad only said we had to live in the house for a year.

The letter asked if I'd take care of Suzy's situation. I did, through a mediator."

Gabriel had to admit it was a smooth move he hadn't considered. "That was smart."

"Watching you moon around after Laura hasn't been pretty. If you got snagged so easily, it could happen to anyone. I had to measure my risk appetite, and I decided it was pretty low."

"I have not been snagged." Gabriel felt his ill humor returning.

"Then back away from the window," Pete said. "I'm sure she can see you from behind those blinds."

Laura probably could. She'd probably be unsurprised that he was keeping watch over her. He sighed, realized she also wouldn't appreciate it and slid away from the window, feeling silly.

"Again, you could just go say hi." Pete stood, stretching. "Anybody for banana fritters?"

Gabriel frowned. "Fritters? Who's going to make those?"

"Laura said she would since she was coming over. It's either that or we grill burgers. I offered burgers because I'm not exactly a banana man. She said the choice was yours since you'd been through a lot lately. We all agreed that was the case."

His life was out of control, hijacked by people he didn't really know that well. He was thinking about the past, and everybody else seemed happy to go along with the cards Pop had dealt them, singularly unsuspicious about the old man's true motives.

"Burgers," he said, "and I guess I'll ring the damn

dinner bell." Feeling almost relieved, he jerked open the door. Ben jumped to his feet, startled, and Laura stared at him with shock.

"Morgan," Penny said, a sweet smile on her face.

"Are we bothering you?" Laura asked. "Pete and Dane said we could come inside, but we prefer to sit outside. It's a lovely evening."

"Ben," Gabriel said, "what the hell are you doing on my porch, anyway?"

"Got no place to go at the moment." Ben didn't seem too concerned by that. "Your dad bought my place. This is as close to home as I can get."

"But where were you before that?" Gabriel demanded. "You were somewhere, weren't you?" He looked at Laura, who didn't seem that disturbed by his bad manners. Stepping around him, Dane and Pete went to brush leaves and blown dirt off the picnic table and set up the grill for burgers.

Ben scratched his head. "Well, I've sort of been in this town and that town looking for work. Then you boys came back, and I pretty much figured it wouldn't hurt if I hung around here a bit."

"You tried to shoot me." Gabriel wasn't sure how he was supposed to forget about that. Turning the other cheek in this case would be a trifle hard.

"Didn't try too hard, son. I really didn't give it my best shot. And I was under the influence of some booze and self-pity, I don't mind admitting." The old man scratched his head and rubbed his chin ruefully. "Sorry I scared you, though. Won't happen again. I gave your brothers my word."

"I wasn't scared. It's against the law to take potshots at people." Gabriel felt annoyance rising inside him. This was not a Hallmark card moment, never would be for him. Anger and mistrust were wrung up together inside him. Why did he get the feeling that this new family was being thrust upon him? "I don't trust you, Ben, to be perfectly honest."

"I respect that," Ben said calmly, "but on the bright side, it's not like I'm in the running to be your father-in-law or anything."

Pete and Dane swung around to stare at them. Laura's eyes went huge. The words hung silent and awkward in the twilight air.

Ben glanced around at everyone. "Well, I'm not," Ben reiterated, "so there's the bright side, right?"

It would be hell having Ben for a father-in-law. Whatever foolish daydreams he'd had concerning Laura were blown to dust. He should never have kissed her, should never have toyed with her affections.

Now that she and her father were coming to some type of reunion, he could excuse himself from the picture-perfect moment he didn't want to be painted into. "Think I'll go check on the horses. Good night." He headed off, leaving everyone else to enjoy what had become a family picnic.

Almost.

LAURA STARED AFTER GABRIEL, disappointed by his reaction. She could feel his withdrawal from the gathering, from her. Even from the children, and that hurt the most. He was big and strong and caring, and she had kept him at arm's length. There were reasons for that, but she didn't want him resenting her, or her father.

Although it was easy to resent Ben. He had lost his temper. No one would forgive someone who shot at them.

"I've made a mess of this," Ben said sadly. "I'm never touching another drop of drink."

Dane and Pete went back to scrubbing off the grill. It looked like it hadn't been scrubbed properly or even used in years. "Listen, Ben," she said, sitting down on the porch beside him, "it's great that you're not going to drink anymore. It's great for you, it's great for the kids. You might even consider some counseling or A.A. In the meantime, don't worry about Gabriel. There was nothing to mess up."

"I was just so mad thinking Josiah had cheated me. I always hated getting cheated." Ben sniffed, rubbing his nose on his shirt. "Josiah is a tricky one, too. He's a smart man. He didn't get so wealthy by being a sucker." He sighed deeply. "Unlike me."

"This is the time to stop feeling sorry for yourself, don't you think, Ben?" She shifted Perrin in her arms; Penny sat quietly between them. "If you see yourself as a victim, then you'll be one."

He slowly nodded. "I guess I fell into that trap when your mother went away. I thought she was happy with me. Never dreamed she'd go off."

Laura had read the letter from her mother many times over the years. She'd long since made peace with the fact that her mother hadn't been able to handle life with a drifter who moved from town to town. She'd gone back north where she had friends. It wasn't that she didn't love her baby, she'd said in the letter. She just felt Ben would be the better parent.

It had been like being given up for adoption. Painful in the growing years, hard as a teenager and probably contributing to Laura's desire to marry a kind, gentle man who seemed solid as a rock, someone who'd be there for her forever. "Ben, it's all right about Mom. We did fine on our own."

"I've been an ass." He looked down at Penny, who stared up at his whiskered face without judgment. "I'm sorry I was hard on your husband, Laura. When he died, I relapsed. I blamed myself for letting my stubbornness get between us."

The familiar knife of pain went through Laura at all the time wasted between them, when Dave had been alive, when her father could have been part of their family. It was time that could never be replaced.

"And now I've shot at your new boyfriend and ruined things for you," he said. "He's never going to want me around."

"Gabriel's not my boyfriend," Laura said firmly, "and if you're sincere about quitting drinking, I want you around and that's all that matters."

He nodded, glancing at Penny and Perrin wistfully. "I am."

"And no more feeling sorry for yourself."

"No." He shook his head. "I've got a lot to live for now."

"And you forget about that oil business you think Josiah pulled over on you," she said sternly.

A grimace wrinkled his face. "That's a little more

difficult. A man hates to have something taken from him."

"I don't think there's anything here. There'd be drillers out here if there was. And do you know what the start-up costs on an operation like that would be?" She looked at her father sincerely. "Unless it was an oil find the size of, I don't know, something in the Gulf, it probably wouldn't be worth the drilling costs."

He blinked. "You're right."

She nodded.

He thought about that for a minute. "But why'd he give you all that money for the kids if it wasn't guilt money?"

"Because Mr. Morgan was a nice old man."

Ben shook his head. "No, Josiah Morgan is not."

"It doesn't matter, does it? He felt like he could help our family when Dave died. That's a good thing, isn't it?"

Ben glanced over at Dane and Pete. "He couldn't get along with his own family, though. Never did understand how that came to pass."

"It's none of our business. People probably say the same thing about us." She kissed Perrin and Penny on their heads.

"Hamburgers? Or hot dogs?" Pete asked. "What does everyone want?"

Laura stood, feeling awkward. "I'm not sure we should stay for dinner. Gabriel made his feelings about our presence pretty plain."

Pete grinned at her. "Gabriel was always the slow child among us. He'll cool off in a bit."

Dane laughed, overhearing his brother's comment. "Besides Jack, he's definitely the most temperamental."

She sat Penny at the picnic table. Somewhat sheepishly, Ben sat down beside Penny.

"It's awfully nice of you boys to forgive me," Ben said.

"You don't have to sing for your supper, Ben," Dane said kindly. "Let's just enjoy the wonderful summer evening."

"Every one of us here is a sinner," Pete added, plopping a big juicy burger in front of Ben. A hot dog followed for Penny, and then a burger for Laura. Perrin sat in her lap, watching everything with big eyes and his fist in his mouth.

"It's a bit charred because we overfired the grill. We'll get better in time," Dane said.

Dane and Pete served themselves, then sat across from Ben and Laura. "I'll say a blessing," Pete offered, and they all bowed their heads until they heard the back door slam.

They glanced up to see Gabriel standing in the doorway.

"The prodigal brother returns," Pete said. "Grab a burger."

Gabriel looked at the picnic table, divided with Laura's family on one side, the Morgans on the other. He had no appetite, except maybe for Laura, something he'd discovered that was growing in spite of his objection to those emotions. "I don't think I'm going to be able to stay here."

They all stared at him.

"Tonight?" Pete asked.

He couldn't meet Laura's steadfast gaze. "At all."

Chapter Seven

Laura's heart sank at Gabriel's words. He obviously had a problem with her family. He definitely did not want them there. She couldn't blame him, either. She held Perrin tighter to her. Maybe she'd made a bad judgment call, believing that because Mr. Morgan had welcomed them, his sons would, too.

"Ben," Gabriel said, "how are you at doing odd jobs on a ranch?"

Ben looked at him. "Could do a good-sized bit of work in my day."

Gabriel folded his arms across his chest. "Are you wanting a job?"

"Depends." Ben jutted out his chin, letting everyone know his pride was at stake.

Gabriel's gaze briefly flicked to Laura. "We've got one open here. This place needs a lot of work."

Ben's jaw sagged. "Do you mean it?" He glanced around at Pete and Dane, whom Laura noticed were staring at Gabriel with approval.

Gabriel nodded. "My brothers feel you could be helpful. You have good knowledge of a working ranch."

It seemed Ben's eyes shone brighter. "I'll take you up on that offer, then."

Gabriel nodded. "You'll have to ask my brothers the particulars of where you should start." He glanced around at the gathering. "Laura, Ben, thank you for coming by." He fondly tousled Penny's and Perrin's hair, surprising Laura. "I'll be heading out."

They all watched in silence as Gabriel left.

"Uh, anybody want pickles with their burgers?" Dane asked to cover the awkward silence. Penny ate her hot dog, and Perrin strained to get down and crawl on the ground. Laura had the strangest sensation that she was missing something in Gabriel's words. He sure hadn't seemed happy. "Can you watch my kids, Ben?" she asked her dad.

"Sure," Ben said, happy to be asked.

Laura handed Perrin to her father, then hurried around to the front of the house so she could catch Gabriel before he departed. He'd said he wasn't going to stick out the year on the ranch—something was bothering him. Badly.

She had to know it wasn't her—or her family.

"Gabriel, wait." She hurried across to where he was backing his truck down the drive. "What is your problem?"

He gazed at her, his eyes pensive. "If I have one, I'm keeping it to myself."

Wasn't that just stubborn as a mule? She shrugged. "I think something's on your mind."

He resumed backing down the drive. She let him go this time, hating his withdrawal. Hiding your emotions was too easy.

She watched him stop his truck, then pull slowly back up the drive, like a magnet moving toward her.

"Maybe we should talk," he said.

"As long as it's your idea," she said sweetly, and got into his truck.

"It wasn't my idea to offer your father a job," he said, heading away from the ranch.

"I thought not. Why did you?"

"My brothers thought we should. And I'm not exactly objective about the situation, considering I don't completely trust him."

"Nor should you," Laura said, not hurt in the least. "He hasn't always been trustworthy." She took a deep breath. "If it makes your decision any easier, I'm taking some leaps of faith where Ben is concerned these days, as well."

"I don't think I'd be able to be friends as easily with my father if he suddenly came back."

She figured that hadn't been an easy admission to make. "I have children, Gabriel. Ben deserves a chance to be a good grandfather, even if he didn't agree with my choice of life partner. That's always going to hurt, but he regrets it now. And I can't wish those years we spent apart never happened, because they did."

"That's one of the things I like about you. You're steadfast." Gabriel glanced toward her briefly. "I just don't think I'll ever be close to my father, especially now that he's got us all tied here for whatever purpose."

"Parenthood isn't easy at any age."

He stopped the truck outside a roadside ice-cream stand. "Would it bother you if you were part of a setup?"

"No, because I don't see myself that way."

Gabriel looked at her. "Even though Josiah gave your kids money, even though he asked me to look after you, you don't see this as part of a grand scheme?" He sighed. "I do. I resent the hell out of it."

She felt prickles run over her skin. "You're safe from me."

"Oh, I know that. You've got an honest-to-God electric fence up around you." Gabriel stared at her so intently she felt her bones turn to water. "It would almost be easier if you didn't."

"Meaning you could sleep with me and then move on? As easily as you're going to move on from your father's request?" She lifted her chin. "I didn't see you as the type of man who looks for the easy way out. Even Ben's got more spirit than that."

Well, that little minx, Gabriel thought. How dare she decide he was spineless? If she knew how badly he wanted to kiss her, shut those pretty lips up so they'd stop taunting him, she'd jump right out of his truck and run back to her safe little family.

He hated indecision, despised fear and inaction. Strength for a man lay in his stubborn attachment to his ideals, and she was shaking every one he had. He hadn't wanted to hire Ben, but part of him knew he'd win approval from her for it. Now he realized how desperately he craved that approval.

But he didn't want to feel this way, not so deeply.

About *any* woman, and no million dollars was worth it. A man worth his salt earned his own damn money, he didn't get paid to go to the altar.

That's what he felt like. That's what he'd really meant when he'd said he might not stick out the year. As ticked as he was at his brothers for making him hire Ben—a problem lodged in his own brain because Pete and Dane seemed to think it was a brilliant plan—he really didn't want to admit his father was controlling his life.

His choice of bride. His will to marry.

Dane, he'd noticed, had to feel the same because he didn't give two flips about who this mysterious Suzy was. "Do you know a Suzy in this town? I believe she may have a few children."

Laura turned big eyes on him. "Suzy? Don't you know, since you're asking about her?"

Gabriel shrugged. "Pop left Dane a letter about someone named Suzy."

"Oh." Laura seemed surprised by that. "She's not exactly his type."

"Really? What type is Dane's?" He watched her, obviously interested in her reply. What made her think she knew his brother at all?

"She has twin baby girls. I'm not certain any of you Morgans would want to take on parenting duties," Laura said slowly, then shook her head. "I see what's bothering you. Your father seemed to have planned to get you brothers women with ready-made families."

"Would be awful devious of him."

She nodded. "What I think you're underestimating

is that he wanted grandchildren and doesn't mind adopting them into his family. I don't think he's actually crazy enough to assume he can induce four hardened bachelors to get to the altar."

"Yeah, Pop is that ornery." He nodded. "As least your father only took a shot at me. Mine's trying to shoot holes in our lives."

"You probably learned a lot about being bullet-proof in the military," she said smoothly. "But your father wants the same thing mine does—to be close to his family. And if he uses money or connections to make that happen, can you blame him? He's not getting any younger."

"I prefer the direct approach."

She shook her head. "No, you don't. You've been running from me ever since you kissed me."

That was certainly direct coming from a young widow with children. "I've been trying not to do it again. You didn't seem too happy about it, and a gentleman respects a lady's wishes."

"I do appreciate you hiring my father, Gabriel. I saw something come into his eyes I haven't seen in years. I think it was hope. He seems to be changing."

"Wasn't easy. He's made an ass of himself."

She tapped his hand, which was resting on the steering wheel. "All of us probably have. I doubt he'll let you down, though."

"Hope not," he grumbled.

"So you've done what your father asked of you. You've watched out for me, employed my dad. You can go on with your life now and not worry about me."

"It's not that easy," Gabriel said with reluctance. "Your kids have gotten under my skin."

Laura looked at him. "What do you mean?"

"See, this is the part I wasn't expecting," he said, realizing all of a sudden what he hadn't been able to put into words before. "I didn't expect to find myself caring about your children."

She seemed to withdraw from him. He knew he had headed into deep water, and there was no going back to shore. "Guess I see why Pop liked them so much. Penny's adorable and Perrin…I hate it when he cries. He makes me want to comfort him."

Her face was a blank he couldn't read.

"It's okay," he said, steeling his heart. "I just find myself thinking about them…and even if I wanted to leave, I don't think I could leave *them*."

Laura didn't know what to say. Perhaps Gabriel was only offering himself in a brotherly capacity. He didn't act like a man who was interested in her—beyond that initial quick kiss, he hadn't made a move toward her.

He wouldn't. Behind that wolf's coat hid a chivalrous heart. Just like his father, just like his brothers. These men all walked dangerous paths, but they wanted the heart and soul of life: family, friends, community.

They just didn't want to admit it.

"If you're offering to take a man's role in my children's lives, I wouldn't turn that down," Laura said. "Mason spends a lot of time with them, and—"

He took her hand in his. Laura stopped speaking, held herself stiffly. Nothing in her body would relax.

Gently, he pressed her palm to his lips. His eyes were dark and fathomless.

Oh, boy. She was pretty sure he wasn't thinking "uncle" now. Her heart beat too hard; her breath went shallow. She couldn't take her hand away from his warm lips. She couldn't think. She felt herself falling under Gabriel's spell, falling faster than she'd ever fallen in her life. There was nothing safe here; this was not a gentle friendship he was offering.

She knew he was waiting for her to speak. A man like him would probably only offer his protection once…and yet, she could not reach into the flames to feel the desire he was offering to ignite.

She lowered her gaze, her pulse racing. After a moment, he put her hand in her lap and rolled down his window. "Ice cream?" he asked, his tone respectful.

"No, thank you."

"Think I'll get a limeade." He pressed the button, placed an order for two and stared out the front window pensively.

"Gabriel, I—"

"You know," he said, "I'll always be here for you, no matter what."

"For a year."

He nodded.

"Because your father asked you to watch out for me."

He turned to look at her. "It won't hurt me to spend time around your children. I know how to observe the boundaries you've set."

It was over, whatever he'd been offering her a

moment ago. "Thank you," she said, her heart jumping too hard.

He nodded, paid for the order when a carhop brought them and handed Laura a drink.

"No problem," he said. "No problem at all."

Chapter Eight

Man, he was a sap.

Gabriel decided his life was a runaway train driven by his father. He'd hired his enemy, fallen for the man's daughter and her kids. He was changing, being changed and he wasn't sure he liked it. "If we head back now, we can still grab some of those burgers."

"So you're staying in Union Junction?"

"As long as you and I can avoid my father's manipulation, I can probably survive."

She nodded. "I need to put Perrin to bed. It was nice of your brothers to invite us over, though."

Yeah, they'd shanghaied him on that one. "So, back to this Suzy."

He felt her gaze on him as he drove.

"She's a nice lady. Rides a lot."

He grunted. Dane wasn't usually cut out for nice ladies—that had the sound of commitment and wedding bells tied to it. "What did Pop feel he owed her?"

"I don't know." She adjusted her seat belt, then quit

fidgeting. "Have you ever considered going over to France to talk to your father?"

"Hell, no. Didn't talk to him in America, sure as hell aren't going to cross the world to do it." Why would he, anyway? They hadn't had anything to say to each other in years.

"So what was it exactly that happened? Do you mind me asking?"

He did mind, but since it was Laura, he could tolerate the question. "There's no easy answer, other than we all got tired of being on the rough side of Pop's tongue." It had been hard facing constant criticism. None of them had ever lived up to Pop's ideals. "Pop was a hard taskmaster."

"I know. It's how he made his money."

"I guess. But his way wasn't my way, nor Dane's, nor Pete's and sure as hell not Jack's." If there was ever a man who'd had all his ambition for steady living driven out of him, it was Jack. Jack was perfectly suited to rodeo because it was a gamble, a walk on the wild side. Just man pitted against beast and a score that determined the outcome.

In other words, it was pretty much a day-to-day test of survival skills. "Beyond the fact we couldn't please Pop and we knew he'd never be proud of us, we did something he just couldn't tolerate. We knew he'd never forgive us, so we left. Unfortunately, when we left, none of us felt good about it, so we sort of drifted apart. Ten years moves a lot faster than you think it might. People say they get busy and they do, but it's just all noise for the relationships they're avoiding."

"Oh, I know how fast time can slip away."

Damn, he'd sounded like he was preaching. "We were pretty much of a handful for Pop to raise. Chafing against authority and all that."

She smiled. "As a teacher, I have to ask if you did well in school."

"None of us did particularly well in regular school. All of us enlisted except Jack, and from there we found our own niches. I'm proud to say that the military put me through four years of college, and then I made top grades."

"Good for you."

"Yeah." He hadn't had Pop chewing on him to do well, so he'd done it for himself. "So then I served out the rest of my time and now I'm answering the call to family duty."

"Very honorable."

"Not really, I guess. Just trying to beat Pop at his own game."

She laughed. "I don't think you realize how much he's mellowed in his old age."

He grunted.

"And I don't really believe the reason you're doing all this is because you're trying to best your father," she said, "because that would mean you still care very much about his opinion, and you don't. Do you?"

Ah, she was being sneaky. He liked that. "Not sure."

"I know families can be messy. I also believe it's best to let the past go if possible. Even if you felt your father was never proud of you, you're proud of your choices. You're your own man."

"You're a regular mind reader, aren't you?" He wasn't sure he liked her picking at his emotions.

"Teachers do some of that," she said coolly, "but having known your father, I know that he isn't a man who is truly comfortable with his emotions. Most people aren't."

He stopped at the ranch. "I'd better feed you a hamburger before you blow a circuit."

She smiled and got out of the truck. "Do you feel better now that you've cooled off some?"

"Maybe." He stared down at her, thinking he wasn't cool at all. He was on a slow boil around Laura.

"Just don't say you're not going to stick out the year again, at least not because of me." She looked up at him with those endless eyes, and he felt his resistance melting. "You're as easy to get attached to as your father, you know," she told him.

He didn't know what to make of that. Or her. He shook his head and followed her around to the back patio.

Ben was enjoying his grandkids. Pete and Dane were throwing a Frisbee around, and not too well, either. Gabriel scowled at the makeshift family gathering.

Then he looked at Perrin and Penny and broke out in a grin. They were cute, unafraid of Ben. He wasn't sure he could ever forgive Ben—the man could have killed him in a drunken stupor—but Laura was right. It would be better for Penny and Perrin if their grandfather was active in their lives.

If Ben was serious about turning his life around.

"I really do appreciate the job," Ben told him, his eyes shining over the heads of his grandchildren. "Feel like I have a purpose now. Your brothers told me I can start tomorrow."

"Great," Gabriel said, his voice stern. "You have to lock your guns in a gun cabinet or get rid of them altogether now that you've got grandkids. Even BB guns, air rifles, pellet guns. Hell, even water guns." He jutted out his chin.

The Frisbee landed on the grass. Pete and Dane stared at him. Laura nodded.

"He's right, Dad. It's a good idea."

Her gaze met Gabriel's. He knew she understood that he might not ever trust Ben, but she also thought he was trying to be cool about what happened. A man had a right to be ticked about being shot at, didn't he?

"It was a BB gun and he was far away," Pete told him. "Not that it couldn't have harmed you but we're not talking the need for a bulletproof vest, either, bro."

"Yeah, well." He'd been in the military too long to appreciate someone aiming a gun at him. Any kind of accident could happen with toddlers around. "For that matter, we're locking ours away in the attic. I don't think that's too cautious, do you?" He couldn't stand the thought of Penny and Perrin accidentally getting near a hunting rifle or…his chest constricted, his mouth went dry. Clearly his brothers thought he had gone mental, then they shrugged and went on with their game. Laura watched him, her expression concerned, but with a soft smile on her face. His mind raced, still on Penny and

Perrin. There was a pond on the property, knives in the kitchen. The fireplace had sharp corners on it where Perrin could fall and hurt himself. There were two staircases that the children could tumble down. Acres of farmland surrounded them. He scanned the perimeter of the property, thinking that if one of the children wandered away, he wasn't sure they could find them easily.

He realized he was panicked. He could count on one hand the times he'd been scared in the military, and that was when he'd been in a war zone.

He couldn't imagine actually being a parent.

"Are you all right, Gabriel?" Laura asked.

He was beginning to wonder.

DANE WAS WONDERING, TOO, mostly what was eating at Gabriel. He jerked his head at Pete and they slipped inside the house. From the kitchen, they watched Laura and Ben play with the grandkids, and Gabriel hover nearby like an uncertain bear.

"Think he likes her?" Dane asked.

"Pop probably hoped he would."

They sprawled in the wooden, rounded-back chairs set at six places around the table. "There were four of us, and Pop. Guess we never needed the sixth chair unless we had company." Dane remembered they all used to toss their coats in the sixth chair, and Pop had gotten so mad.

"If he gets married before his year is up, does that mean he forfeits if he moves away?" Dane was thinking that if Gabriel wasn't open to getting serious, he was probably crazy. Laura was a beautiful woman. She was sweet. Her kids were great. He didn't give Pop much credit for anything, but he'd certainly picked a nice family to associate himself with.

"I don't know." Pete shook his head. "No one knows but Pop. I wouldn't say that to Gabriel, though."

"Oh, hell no. Although he did consider leaving, briefly."

Pete laughed. "He hates being boxed in. Even when he was a kid, he hated being told what to do."

"So do I." They were all stubborn chips off the block like their dad. "Wonder why Pop never remarried if he was so set on family."

They sat quietly, listening to Gabriel and Laura calling to Penny as they tried to teach her to throw the Frisbee.

"Dunno. Didn't he always say marriage was for suckers?" Pete kicked his boots up onto a chair.

"He did." He'd been pretty bitter when their mom left. Refused to speak of her for years. "So if it's for suckers, he'll understand none of us choosing to settle down."

They heard Perrin's happy squeal, saw Ben go by the window holding his grandchild.

"Maybe one house can only hold so much bitterness," Pete said. "I don't understand why Pop didn't match me to a bride."

"Hey!" Dane sat up. "This Suzy girl is not my match!"

Laura came inside the kitchen, smiling when she saw them relaxing at the table. "Too much activity out there for you boys? You're not used to being around children. They can be overwhelming."

"I can handle it," Dane said.

"That's good." She got out glasses and a tumbler. "Gabriel says you're supposed to meet with Suzy Winterstone at some point? She has darling twins." She filled the pitcher with water and ice.

Dane sat up. "How old?"

"About twelve months old. Why?" She glanced at him curiously.

"Where's the father?" His mouth felt completely dry. Damn Pop! He could almost feel a trap ensnaring him.

"There isn't one. Well, not in residence anyway. Suzy had a boyfriend. She thought they were serious, but apparently, he wasn't. She's not heard from him since he went back to Australia or wherever he was from. Mr. Morgan hired a couple of nannies to help her and now they're doing just fine."

"Nannies?" Dane didn't really know what a nanny did. Didn't they just push around big fluffy strollers with oversized wheels?

"Well, she has the money to have help. Definitely having two children at once is challenging. And being alone would be hard. Plus, she had a C-section that had some complications."

"But if she has money, then she doesn't need…like, a man or anything." Dane knew he sounded like he was desperate to run away from the situation, and he was, but he didn't want to sound completely unchivalrous.

"She has money because of your father's generosity."

She took the tray of drinks outside, leaving Dane to stare at Pete.

"Pretty weird hobby Pop had."

"So was collecting huge acreages. Made him a lot of money, though." Pete sounded untroubled by that.

"You're just not worried because you didn't get a letter of doom." Dane felt annoyed by that. "Maybe Pop only felt that Gabriel and I were suitable choices for—"

"His schemes. I'd buy that. You guys are the youngest. And the most impressionable."

Dane shook his head. "I don't need a woman with two babies. That sounds high maintenance."

Pete laughed. "So is Pop."

LAURA STAYED LATER THAN she'd planned, watching Ben play with her children, feeling like her life was a completed circle now. Wholeness eased her heart. Penny and Perrin would have a father figure to look up to; Ben appeared to have a new lease on life.

She could forget the past. Not Dave, of course. Her heart still burned with sadness when she thought about him. But healing old pain made her feel brighter about everything. It was the start of summer, a great time for new beginnings.

Gabriel made her feel a snap of excitement, too, as much as she didn't want him to be part of her emotional healing process. With Ben in their lives, the father-figure gap she'd worried about would be alleviated.

She stood. "I have to take the children home and put them to bed. Thank you for a lovely evening."

Penny tiredly rubbed her eyes; Perrin's were drifting shut as he lay against Gabriel's chest. Gabriel and Ben followed her as she picked Penny up and walked her to the car.

"I'll be by tomorrow," Ben said eagerly. "We could take the kids for a ride into town. I'd like to show them off to my buddies."

Laura smiled. "They'd love that."

Ben glanced at Gabriel self-consciously, then said, "Thanks for everything, Morgan."

Gabriel watched as Ben ambled away. "I can't get used to people calling me that in my father's house."

She strapped Penny into her car seat, then took Perrin from Gabriel to do the same. "What did they call you in the service?"

"Morgan. But I hear it here, and I look around for Pop."

"It took me a few weeks to get used to being Mrs. Adams."

It was then that the idea hit Gabriel, blooming big in his brain, like facing the worst fear he'd ever had.

Chapter Nine

"Try getting used to Mrs. Morgan," Gabriel said.

Laura turned around. "What do you mean?"

"It could be your name. For a year, anyway."

Her heart skipped strangely inside her. She wanted to run and hide in the worst way. "I don't want a husband."

"I don't want a wife in the traditional sense. But it wouldn't kill me to have some help making this year more bearable, I'll admit."

She sank into the seat and closed the car door. "I have to get my kids home."

He nodded, his eyes dark, his gaze unfathomable, before his attention switched to the kids in the backseat. "They look like they've had a full day. I'm glad I got to see them."

She hesitated, Gabriel's words just sinking in. "I'm sorry, but did you just propose to me?"

"I am proposing, yes. You can call it a business proposal, a merger or an idea to make my life easier. Whatever you want to call it."

She shook her head. "You are your father's son."

"Laura, I understand that you're still grieving. Whatever limits you'd want on a partnership between us would be fine by me."

She felt her fingers tremble. He didn't understand that she wasn't that much of a daredevil. Besides the obvious thrill of being married to a man like Gabriel, she wouldn't be able to count on the snuggling, the gentle companionship that Dave had offered.

"Just think about it for now. The option's open. Good night, kids." He reached through the window and touched each child's hand. "See you tomorrow."

She backed up the car and drove away, her mind whirling over Gabriel's proposal. She didn't want to get married. He didn't want to get married.

The only reason he'd asked her was because of his father. It had something to do with the wager his father had set upon his sons.

On the other hand, Gabriel really seemed to enjoy her children. He had even offered Ben a job, which she knew was against his better judgment, and maybe even hers. But the fact that he'd been willing to give her father a chance caught her attention. Sometimes a chance was all someone needed to start over, jump into better luck.

Her eyes widened as she realized he was giving her a chance, much like he had Ben. Gabriel was a giver, hiding behind a gruff exterior. She'd been fooled—or frightened—by his seeming harshness.

Marriage to him would be a business, just like everything else in the Morgan family. Because of their father, they couldn't help but think coolly, strategically.

She missed Dave's uncomplicated style. Day by day, come what may.

However, that lifestyle had led to being alone with two small children and financial hardship. Had it not been for Josiah Morgan—who'd seen fit to give her a chance—she'd still be knocked off her feet.

She was surprised to find herself mulling Gabriel's offer.

The temptation shocked her.

Her gaze found Penny and Perrin in the backseat through the rearview mirror, and she knew she was looking at the one reason she would consider Gabriel's offer. A chance for a wonderful father for her children didn't come along that often. Maybe she was being selfish, but secretly she longed for that chance for them.

It didn't hurt that Gabriel was sexier than any man had a right to be.

WHATEVER LABEL ANYONE wanted to put on marriage—partnership or love at first sight—Gabriel had never considered the option. He was too old to be fooled by sexual attraction, but he was insanely attracted to the little mother. Nor did he care that he was falling into his father's plan willingly.

Fact was, he didn't give a damn what his father or his brothers thought. He liked Penny and Perrin. He liked Laura. The piece of his life they'd begun to occupy felt like home to him, and he was smart enough to realize that all the houses and land Pop had acquired over the years were probably a filler for the feeling of home.

Bottom line, a man shouldn't be so dumb he let his pride rule him.

He knew Laura probably would never love him. Actually, his chances weren't great on that score, since she was still in love with her deceased husband. He understood, but he didn't mind waiting that out. The desire to own that piece of life they'd embedded in his heart, that intangible thing he'd craved all his life, was simply too strong. He was a risk taker; he wasn't afraid of it. In fact, he almost relished the challenge.

A great chunk of the challenge—and he wasn't afraid to admit it—was that he'd never planned to have children of his own. But he could be a father to two kids who needed one—at least he could try. This was the toughest part of proposing marriage: not knowing if he could be an adequate father. It required settling down for real commitment. Living in one town. This town.

And what if they stayed married beyond the year he needed to put in at the ranch? Little League, dance recitals, trying not to beat on teenage boys who would come to date his daughter, learning golf with his son. Golf was probably a good thing to learn, he mused. He'd have to attend church with them, something he had refused to do. God had been a very far away component of his life in the world's hidden outposts.

He'd have to change a lot about himself. Being a parent required sacrifice. He wasn't afraid of sacrifice.

But the reality that he might let them down sent sweat trickling down the back of his neck. He'd had a stern role model for fatherhood—he hoped Laura didn't factor that into her consideration of his proposal.

He really craved the piece of home she represented.

"Home, sweet home!"

The bellow from the foyer at 5:00 a.m. shot Gabriel upright in his bed. The voice was a nightmare; he remembered the lashing roughness of it.

It couldn't be. He'd simply had a nightmare.

He heard familiar heavy boots clomping on the hardwood floor downstairs. His pulse rate jacked up. He went to stare over the rail. Dane and Pete met him there.

Suddenly he was an awkward teenager again, wishing he didn't have to face the critical appraisal of his father. "What the hell, Pop?" he demanded.

The white-haired and strong Josiah Morgan looked up at his three sons. "I see money *can* buy a man everything." His weathered face folded into a frown. "Except Jack. Where the hell is Jack?"

"Not being bought," Gabriel replied. "Helluva price to pay for a family reunion, if that's what you wanted."

His father shrugged. "A good businessman checks up on his investments."

"I'm leaving," Dane said under his breath. "I don't need this crap."

Pete nodded. "Damn if he doesn't make me remember all over again how much I despise him. Old goat."

"Shh," Gabriel said. "Don't disrespect the chance to learn from life's mistakes."

"Are you crazy?" Pete asked. "The man isn't a father. He's a human computer."

"Maybe he can be reprogrammed."

"I don't care," Pete said. Their father ignored them,

headed into the kitchen. They could hear his boots striding through to the den. "He doesn't own me."

"If Ben can turn over a new leaf, it's possible Pop can, too." Gabriel wasn't going to run from his father's dark bitterness. "He wouldn't be here if he wasn't up to something. Wasn't it you who said we should keep our enemy tucked close to our chest?"

"Yeah, but that was when it was your ass in hot water," Pete said, and Dane nodded.

"I personally don't believe in that enemy theory," Dane said. "It isn't the way I handled being a Ranger."

"I preferred distance between me and the enemy. The old saw about close enough for hand grenades worked for me," Pete said.

"God hates a coward." Gabriel turned to go downstairs to face his father.

"Nope, God gave me legs to depart." Dane shrugged. "I don't have a big enough shovel for all the crap Pop's gonna give us. And it ticks me off that he lured us here under false pretenses. He just wanted us home."

"I agree with Dane. I'm too old to be trapped into one of Pop's sorry-ass confrontations. His approval hasn't mattered to me in years. Gabriel, you're on your own if you're fool enough to stay." Pete went to his room.

Gabriel figured he was used to that. Hell, they all were. "Well, maybe Pop's carping won't bother me as much as it would you. Otherwise, my backup plan for getting along with Pop is to get married," he said, and grinned when his brothers stuck their heads back into the hall.

"Married?" Pete repeated.

Gabriel nodded. "I asked Laura to marry me."

"Whoa," Dane said, "you're setting a bad precedent here. Do not think that I intend to do the same. In fact, I tore up Pop's letter about that Suzy chick. I'll be telling him that before I leave, too."

"Why are you falling in line with Pop's scheming?" Pete demanded. "This isn't the military, you know. You don't have to jump when sarge commands. Once Pop knows he can buy you, you'll be screwed."

"I'm doing it because Laura needs me," Gabriel said, "although Laura would disagree." Actually that reason was too simplified, but he wasn't going to pour his heart out to his boneheaded brothers. They'd never understand.

"Well, probably no one can save you," Pete said. "Good luck."

"Yeah. Let me know where to send a gift," Dane said.

Gabriel replied, "Here, of course. I'm sticking out my year like I planned."

"With Pop in residence? Does Laura know?" Pete asked. His expression said Gabriel was nuts.

"Doesn't matter to me if Pop's here or not. Doesn't matter to me what Pop thinks about my marriage proposal." Gabriel's heart was singing at the freedom of not caring anymore. "To be honest, I couldn't care less. Everything is in the past and that's where it's going to stay."

"The optimism of a baby," Dane said. "I hope you know what you're doing."

Gabriel shrugged and went downstairs. "So. What ill wind blew you in?"

His father looked up. "How the hell was I to know my place was being looked after?"

"You knew I'd be here. I'd bet you expected all of us to be here." Gabriel slung himself into a leather chair opposite his father. For being apart ten years, he couldn't say there was an outpouring of emotion at the reunion. Nor had the old man changed much. He was craggier, whiter of hair, maybe, but still looked strong as a bull and was obviously marching to his own drummer. "You set this all up knowing we'd all do what you wanted."

"I wish it were that easy." Josiah looked at him. "Are you still in the military?"

"Did my time. Now I'm house-sitting for you."

"Mooching off me, you mean," Josiah said sourly.

"Okay," Gabriel said easily, rising to his feet. "I didn't realize you regretted your own scheme. Ben will be arriving every morning at 5:00 a.m. to water and feed the horses you left for the neighbors to look after."

"Ben? Ben Smith?"

Gabriel nodded. "You said you owed him something. So we gave him a job."

"No one consulted me." Josiah's brows pulled together. "The man is a leech."

"Well," Gabriel said, putting on a hat, "fire him if you want, but you'll let Laura down. Those kids of hers are something, aren't they?" he said, not ashamed to be as sly as his father. "I'll be seeing you."

He went out, not listening to the expletives his father unleashed at him. Getting into his truck, he drove deserted country roads for hours. Then he headed to

Laura's. He sat staring at her house, thinking, trying to pull a plan of action together.

He knew she wasn't likely to accept his proposal. But he could use the buffer between him and Pop. Pop liked Laura; she brought out his less antagonistic side.

She opened the door and seemed to hesitate. Then she waved at him to come inside.

He did before she changed her mind.

"I'm glad you came by," Laura said, "because we should probably talk."

That sounded good to him. He slid onto the bar stool she offered and watched as she made lemonade in the small, bright kitchen. "Where are the kids?"

"Napping. They've been tired lately, and I think it's the June heat." She pinched some mint sprigs, and he could smell the sweet green freshness. "The other night, you made me a proposal."

He nodded. He pretty much knew what her answer was going to be. She looked so calm and refreshing in a white top and blue jean shorts, cute sandals. "I probably didn't handle that as well as I should have."

She looked at him. "But you were sincere?"

"Oh, yeah. Definitely."

She took a deep breath. "I'm not going to fall in love with you."

"I know." Still, hearing the words stated so flatly threw a knife into his chest. He knew his odds were slimmer than a crack in a window. He thought about Pop, angry and pissed off at home, and wondered if he'd ever known real love. "I'm not the romantic type who expects notes signed with a heart."

Pain seemed to jump into her eyes. "I'm not looking for romance. In fact, it would bother me if that's what you're looking for. I just don't have that emotion available to me right now."

"I understand."

"I'd like to accept your proposal."

He sat up straight. "You would?"

She nodded, holding his gaze. "With a couple of modifications."

"Name them." Suddenly, his heart was skidding with joy. He didn't care what the qualifications were; he had never wanted anything so much in his life.

"My children," she said, "come first."

"I wouldn't expect anything else."

"You would in a marriage where you'd been my first love. You would have come first. But I understand that you're offering me a proposition that's pretty much cut-and-dried. As a single mother, I'll admit I see benefits to what you're offering."

She had no idea what benefits he'd be getting. A family. A real wife and kids. Okay, maybe not totally real, but close. Closer than he'd ever expected. "What else?"

For a long moment she looked at him, then took a deep breath. "I know that you're supposed to live in your father's house for a year—"

"He's back," Gabriel interrupted. "As far as I can guess, he's nullified his own game. Pop never did like to give up control."

"I know Mr. Morgan's back." She motioned him to follow her into the garden and turned on a baby monitor. They sat an awkward distance away from each other, but at ten o'clock in the morning, there was no moonlight to confuse romance with negotiations. "Everyone knows he's back. He left a generous donation to the church, the library and the school. And then there's that." She pointed, and Gabriel saw a plastic sandbox shaped like a dinosaur and bags of sand. Shovels and buckets lay in a gaily decorated basket nearby.

"I can't figure him out. Pop came in the house snarling like his old self."

"The whole town is reeling this morning from the gifts." She shook her head. "Maybe you four were problem children?"

"Oh, he'd like you to think that. He'd like everyone to see his good, benevolent side. Thing is, it's so much easier to be nice to people on the surface. Family requires time and effort. It requires being close enough to give a damn."

"Which is why I really shouldn't ask this of you," she said, hesitating, "especially since you should be focusing on your father…"

He was afraid she'd get hung up on Pop and do something generous like decide to crawfish out of his marriage proposal. "Let me worry about Josiah."

"You have to live here with us," she said calmly, her tone serious.

He stared at her, his heart instantly shifting into a slow thudding beat. "Here."

She nodded. "I can't take the children from the only home they've ever known, even if it's only for a year."

"I guess you can't." He wouldn't want them uprooted from their security, especially so soon after losing their father.

"I realize doing so would break the agreement between you and your father—"

"He wasn't going to give any of us a million dollars, anyway," Gabriel said. "It was one of his ruses to trap us. Because he can't come right out and ask for what he wants."

Her eyes went wide at the bitterness in his tone. "I don't want to come between family—"

He got up, pulled her to her feet and kissed her on the mouth, long and hard, definitely not allowing her to retreat. She would never be able to say no to this man about anything, she realized, her heart falling.

Gabriel pulled slowly away from their kiss, brushed her cheek with his fingers, stroked her neck with his palms. "Don't mention him again. This is the family I want."

"I just think—"

"No, you don't." Gabriel shook his head. "Thinking about the old man invites decay into my life. I choose you and Penny and Perrin."

"Your father has been giving away a lot of money," Laura said. "Maybe he is sincere. Maybe he's using his money to bring you closer to him."

"Then he has no idea what I really want in life." Gabriel kissed her hand. "Your children come first, and I live here with you. Have I got it?"

She nodded.

He felt happier than he had in a long, long time. "I'll move in after we're married."

"All right."

"We can probably get the marriage license and blood work done in a week—"

"Or we could go to Las Vegas," Laura said quickly.

He blinked. Was she hot for him? He didn't think so. If anything, she looked scared to death. "What about the children?"

"Mimi and Mason would be happy to keep them."

He didn't really want an Elvis wedding, or one away from her children. Penny would make a darling flower girl. Perrin would be a cute ring bearer of sorts. "Are you sure?"

"Definitely. As soon as possible. Just the two of us."

"I'll pick you up tomorrow." He walked to his truck, not feeling good about the arrangement.

It didn't matter. He could wait a couple of days to find out what Mrs. Adams had up her sleeve. She was taking advantage of his offer of marriage for a reason—but she was forgetting who'd raised him. He knew all about ulterior motives, and he wasn't afraid of hers.

He was finally getting a real family of his own.

GABRIEL FIGURED HE'D BUNKED in enough out-of-the-way places that he could sleep in the foreman's cottage overnight. Hell, he could sleep in a barn if it meant staying away from Pop. Why the hell had the old man really returned? He hadn't accomplished anything he'd supposedly wanted; Pete was gone, Dane had high-tailed it and he wasn't providing a sounding board for his father's bitching.

Yep, he'd take the foreman's deserted shack. Unlocking the door with the key hidden in a secret wall crevice, he went inside, glad to be finally alone.

It had been an exciting day. He'd made plane reservations, wedding reservations, had gotten Laura a ring. Of course, he couldn't get married without buying a couple of stuffed animals for his new kids: a soft, fluffy horse for Penny, a paunchy, huggable teddy bear for Perrin. He couldn't wait—he would be a hundred times better father than Pop.

The foreman's shack hadn't changed, and to his relief it wasn't in the terrible condition he'd expected. He and his brothers had spent some happy hours here hiding from their father. They'd used it as a home away from home. Pop had never been able to keep much help around, so the cottage went for long periods of time unoccupied.

He flipped on one of the bedroom lights, and a figure rose from the bed.

"What the hell?" the figure demanded.

Gabriel frowned. "Ben, what the devil are you doing here?"

Ben rubbed his eyes. "Trying to sleep! What are you doing here?"

"This house is on Morgan property," Gabriel reminded him.

"If you want me taking care of your livestock at five a.m., this is my house." Ben stuck out his jaw. "I can't sleep in fields forever."

Gabriel considered that. The man would be his father-in-law tomorrow. He supposed it was churlish of him to begrudge the man a home. "You think you could have asked?"

Ben shrugged. "The door hadn't been opened in probably five years. Didn't figure as it mattered."

It probably didn't. "I'm avoiding Pop."

"You think *you* are?" Ben swung his legs to the side of the bed. "He wouldn't exactly be jumping for joy to find me on his property." He squinted at him. "Did you tell him you hired me?"

"Yeah." Gabriel sank into an old leather chair that had seen better days. "I'd say he wasn't happy, except he wasn't happy about anything. That's sort of the groove he stays stuck in."

"I don't mind sharing the place with you if you'll sleep," Ben said. "Five o'clock comes early, you know, and my bosses are real jackasses." He snickered and slid back in bed. "Nice of them to hire me, though."

Gabriel rubbed his chin. "Yeah, about that, Ben."

"You promised you'd be silent as a mouse," Ben told him. "So far all I hear is yak, yak, yak."

"I'm marrying your daughter tomorrow."

A long pause met his words. Then Ben sat up.

"Nope," he said, "that ain't gonna do."

Chapter Ten

Laura was nervous. Accepting Gabriel's marriage proposal filled her with a strange type of dread. She'd said yes for all the wrong reasons.

Gabriel was a handsome man. He was sexy, the kind of man most women wanted. But there was something she'd kept from him: she was the reason Josiah Morgan had returned.

Mr. Morgan had made her promise that if any of his sons came home to Union Junction, he was to be notified. She didn't know any of the Morgan boys, and innocently, she had thought it was awful the way they never came to visit their father. Maybe she'd even felt a sad yearning for the relationship she lacked with her own father. Because of the gifts Mr. Morgan had given her children, she'd readily agreed to his request.

She hadn't realized how much they despised him— and she hadn't dreamed he meant to return home to confront them. Mr. Morgan's return had driven Gabriel to a marriage proposal. He claimed he wanted the one thing he'd never had: a real family. Children he could love and hold and call his own. Secretly, she couldn't say that she didn't adore the idea that her children would have a father like Gabriel.

She wasn't going to deny to herself that Gabriel didn't make her blood run hot. A fantasy or two or ten had definitely played in her mind, hotter ones than she'd care to admit.

Yet if he knew that Mr. Morgan had planned to return, had basically lured them and she had helped—she was pretty certain it was a betrayal that Gabriel would not be able to forgive.

She wasn't going to tell Gabriel. He had offered marriage for one year. She had been honest, told him that she wouldn't fall in love with him. She'd had love before, knew what it felt like, how deep it lodged in her heart. What she felt now was lust and a desire to have safety for her children, nothing more.

And when Gabriel left in a year, she would tell Penny and Perrin that Gabriel would always be part of their lives. He would, she knew, just as Mr. Morgan remained part of their world.

Gabriel just wouldn't stay in hers.

Knowing that kept the guilt she felt at bay. Even if she felt like a traitor, it had been an innocent mistake. She'd thought she was doing the right thing, and she couldn't change that now.

JOSIAH MORGAN HAD FEW friends. He had no family who cared for him. It was ironic how much he wanted what he couldn't have, when he could buy everything in sight.

An old journal lay open on his desk. Pictures of him

and his wife at their wedding stayed between the pages of the heavy journal; they were slightly grainy with age and wrinkled at the corners. He treasured those two pictures more than anything he owned.

He knew where his wife had gone. With the money he'd accumulated in his life, he'd been able to hire an investigator. Gisella was living in France, in the countryside, with people who remembered her from her childhood. Her own parents were long deceased, but Gisella still fit in to the surroundings of her youth. He would never contact her, but he needed to know where she'd gone.

He'd met Gisella in the military, in London, when he'd been stationed there as a cook. Back then he hadn't had two pounds in his pocket, but Gisella hadn't cared. They'd found plenty of activities to fill their time, and then Jack had been conceived. Head over heels in love, Josiah married Gisella. He smiled, remembering that day. Never had he seen a woman look more beautiful. Nowadays most women wore too much makeup, had their bodies artificially plumped or toned or browned— Gisella had been the salt of the earth.

As soon as he'd gotten out of the military, he'd begun his lifelong habit of acquisition He was determined to deserve this wonderful woman, give her everything she didn't have. It was rough financially while they were married, but she believed in his dreams. She gave him four beautiful sons.

He was moody, struggling with start-up businesses. He was under the weight of trying to deserve the woman he loved. They fought a lot. Gisella hated being left alone on the ranch; she was afraid of the dark.

Their few cattle started disappearing, and Gisella became nervous with fear. Always edgy, afraid for the boys. Terrified for herself.

He was gone on a business trip to Dallas when he got the worried call from Jack. All of eight years old, Jack tried manfully to tell him his mother was gone—in the end, he dissolved into tears that Josiah would never forget hearing him cry. He hurried home, finding the boys were being kept by Ben Smith, whom Gisella had called for help.

He would never, ever forgive Ben Smith for driving his wife to the airport.

It had been years, and he was still mad as hell. Ben told him that Gisella had planned to call a taxi, but he'd driven her to Dallas to try to talk her out of leaving. Gisella had left a babysitter at the house, with instructions to stay with her sons until their father returned.

He could feel his blood boil all over again. Betrayal, by everyone he knew.

The boys would never understand that from that day forward, he had to teach them to be men. They needed to know that life was hard, and there were disappointments. Nothing was easy, nothing was free. Nobody gave a man a single thing, he earned every bit, and if he was smart, he made that lesson the bedrock of his soul.

Josiah shut the journal and stared at it for a long moment. In the journal, he wrote words daily that he wanted his sons to know about him, about their mother. He was aware they disliked him intensely. But they would know that he had loved them, and whether they considered his love too harsh was something they could decide after he was gone.

His kidneys were failing and he had maybe a year, possibly less. He would not take treatment, would not be chained to a machine. Would not show weakness, nor the fatigue that robbed his strength. Not even the depression that came upon him from time to time. A kidney transplant could save him, but that was not an option he chose. There were many more deserving people in the world who had something to live for. He'd been given his own chances to do something good with his life, and God would judge that.

He'd leave the healing to those who deserved it. He'd struck his deal with life, now he was determined to go out with fireworks. He would be no wimpy candle that blew out unresisting at the slightest puff of wind.

"NOPE," BEN SAID, "YOU ain't marrying my daughter. And if that's why you gave me a job, then you can sure as hell shove it, Morgan."

Gabriel threw himself on the sofa and closed his eyes. The sofa was scratchy and old, made of a plaid fabric that had seen better days. It felt lumpy and out of shape, but Gabriel was too tired to care. "Go to sleep, Ben. We'll argue in the morning."

"Morning or night, next week or next year, I ain't giving you my blessing. You damn Morgans ruin everything you touch, and you ain't gonna upset Laura."

"Listen, Ben, you're no angel. And Laura's old enough to make her own decisions."

"That's just like a Morgan, thinking they can bend everybody else to their will. I'm telling you, leave Laura and the kids out of your screwed-up life."

Ben had a point. He had several points, in fact, but nothing was going to stop Gabriel from marrying Laura, not even her own father. He wanted her so badly that he could practically taste her. Desire washed through him, tugging at him, binding him to her in a way he could never explain.

"She deserves a man who can love her," Ben said, standing over him, "and you come from stock that loves no one but themselves."

"It's not entirely true." Gabriel grimaced.

"Yes, it is. Your whole clan turns on each other at the snap of a finger. Where are your brothers?"

"Not here."

"And how many words have you spoken to your father?"

"Under fifty, maybe," Gabriel admitted.

"Which is why you're hiding out here, and why you're trying to rope my daughter into marrying you. Fact is, you're doing this to get your father's approval."

Gabriel blinked. "You could have a point."

"Yeah. I do. You know your father provided for my grandchildren. So what do you do? You go and ask their mother to marry you. You haven't even known Laura a week. It's not love at first sight or something romantic like that—it's trophy bagging. Like she's some kind of prized deer you can brag that you shot."

"Hey!" Gabriel jerked up on the sofa. "Ben, shut your mouth before I shut it for you. That's a terrible way to talk about your daughter!" There might have been some family psychology at work—he didn't mind admitting that Laura represented wholeness and a sense of family he craved—but he would never see her as a trophy.

Ben stuck out his chin belligerently. "I'm talking about you, not my daughter. You're the hunter here. She's just the innocent prey in your quest for game."

Gabriel shook his head. "I don't know what to say, except you sort of worry me. Didn't you act up about Laura's first husband?"

Ben raised a finger, wagging it at Gabriel. "He wasn't good enough for Laura."

"Is anybody?" Gabriel honestly wanted to know.

"Probably not," Ben barked. "She hasn't yet met the man who deserves her. But I don't expect you to understand that, because you're your father's son."

Gabriel sighed. "Ben, you gotta calm down. It's going to be hard to share Christmas dinners if you talk like that all the time."

"I'm being honest."

"And I appreciate that, but I'm not the devil. And Laura's a smart woman. She wouldn't have said yes if she didn't think marrying me had some merit."

Ben snorted. "Laura is a grieving widow. She thinks you'll be a good father. Maybe you can be, but maybe you won't be. But, son, I know more about you and your family than you'll ever know, and I'll be willing to bet you've never had a relationship with a woman that lasted a year."

Gabriel's brows furrowed.

"Have you?" Ben demanded.

"How do my past relationships affect my future ability to be a good husband?"

Ben put a boot on the side of the sofa and leaned close. "Rumor has it you and your brothers make sport of women."

"Not true," Gabriel said defensively. "While I can't speak for my brothers, I can't exactly say I personally ever met the woman I wanted to spend my life with."

"And did you tell my daughter you planned to stay with her for the long haul?" Ben asked. "I'm just curious, because marriage is a long-term thing. It's a commitment. Something I haven't ever known you Morgans to be good with."

"I was in the military. Can't think of a more demanding commitment than that."

"That's a paycheck. It was also an escape from your father." Ben left the room, heading back to his own exile. "Marriage should not be an escape route, Morgan."

He closed his eyes. "True," he muttered. "I'll take it under advisement."

"I'll be saying the same to Laura."

"Probably a good idea." He'd be worried about having himself for a son-in-law if he was in Ben's boots. Why had he even mentioned it to Ben?

He stared up into the darkness, examining his conscience. It was traditional to ask a father for his daughter's hand in marriage. Perhaps he'd hoped for his future father-in-law's blessing. He really cared about Laura and her family, and that included Ben to some degree. He didn't blame Ben for feeling the way he did.

Yet Gabriel knew he was marrying Laura—unless she changed her mind about having him. He briefly considered tying Ben to his bunk, at least until the *I dos* were spoken, but the old man had a right to do his damnedest. It didn't matter what Ben did, anyway. Laura had said yes, and she wasn't the kind of woman to go back on her word.

Chapter Eleven

"I'm getting married," Gabriel told his father the next day before he left to pick up Laura on the way to the airport. "I know news travels fast here, so I wanted you to hear it from me." He figured Ben had probably already run a marathon to tell his old man, but Josiah looked surprised.

"You are?"

Gabriel nodded. "I'm marrying Laura in Las Vegas today. We'll be back by nightfall."

Josiah's brows beetled. "Not much of a honeymoon."

Gabriel shrugged. "She has two young children. She'd rather not leave them long." He wouldn't tell his father they didn't need any real *honeymooning*.

"Penny and Perrin would be fine with me. They like me," Josiah offered.

"Thanks. But Laura's got her heart set on coming home."

Josiah grunted. "Your brothers slunk out of here without saying much to me. Guess you'd be gone, too, if it wasn't for Laura and the kids."

He probably would. Pop's gaze was on him, inspecting him, waiting for an answer. What was the right answer? What did Pop want to hear? He didn't know. "Since you're back, you can take care of the place yourself, right? And you've got Ben."

Josiah scowled. "I don't need Ben."

"Well, get along with him." Gabriel tossed some stuff into his truck. "I probably won't be seeing you for a while."

"You probably won't. I'm planning on going back to France early next week."

Gabriel turned to look at his father. "Why did you really come home?"

Josiah shook his head. "It's my house, isn't it?"

"So what was the deal about the million dollars if we stayed here for a year?"

Josiah fixed dark eyes on him. "None of you seem to be planning to do it, so what does it matter?"

True enough. Gabriel knew his father had simply been moving them around like chess pieces.

"Gabriel, I have to admit I'm glad you and Laura are getting married."

"I guess so. It makes you a grandfather. Wasn't that what this was all about?" Gabriel felt a little bitter about satisfying one of his father's desires, the familiar resentment welling up inside him that Josiah Morgan was always behind every move in his life.

"Actually, I never dreamed she'd have you," Josiah said. "She was pretty torn up when Dave died. I just wanted you to look after her and the kids while I was gone."

"Did you cheat Ben on purpose?"

Josiah frowned. "I saw value in something that Mr. Smith did not. Including his own family, I might add."

He had a point. But that didn't make it right with Gabriel.

"Pop, have you ever thought that maybe you shouldn't capitalize on people's weaknesses?"

"Hell, no. It's a dog-eat-dog world. Don't kid yourself."

Gabriel shook his head. "Listen, I've got to head out."

He looked at the man who was his father, and yet who felt like he was something else: judge, jury, prosecutor. Time had stretched the bonds between them and deepened the scars. He didn't think either of them would really ever heal the wounds.

"Gabriel, thanks for telling me about the wedding." Josiah turned to go inside his house. For just a moment, Gabriel felt sorry for his father, then decided it was a wasted emotion. Josiah played by his own rules, and they were rules he was comfortable with. Gabriel wasn't going to make the mistake of judging his father.

He drove off to pick up his soon-to-be bride, and it belatedly occurred to him that he had received his father's approval. It felt good.

Marrying Laura would feel good. He'd counted the hours since yesterday.

He was going to be a husband and a father. He couldn't wait.

But when he got to Laura's house, she wasn't there. Instead, he found a note taped to the door.

Gabriel, Dad was having chest pains. I've taken him to the hospital. Laura

LAURA WAS NEARLY SICK WITH fear. Her father looked so pale. Nurses scurried to hook him up to various monitors and an IV. She didn't want him to have a heart attack, she wanted him to be well. Life was short, and she'd wasted time Ben could have had with his grandchildren. She regretted every moment of her stubborn pride.

She should have tried harder to make her father understand how much she loved Dave—although as much as she hated to admit it, Dave hadn't helped to ease Ben's worries. In retrospect, she realized how much Dave's laconic approach to life had worried Ben.

Ben had mumbled how sorry he was that she had to take him to the hospital when she was supposed to be leaving for a wedding in Las Vegas. Laura comforted her father, telling him that everything would work out eventually. She didn't want him upset.

Gabriel strode into the hospital, coming straight to her to close her in his embrace. She allowed herself to be enveloped in his strong warmth, appreciating his caring. "He got sick all of a sudden."

He stroked her hair. "He'll be fine."

She wasn't certain. "I hope so." Through the small window, she could see her father being wheeled down the hall. "It just came on so quickly."

"They'll get him fixed up."

She looked up at Gabriel. "Sorry about the wedding."

"Las Vegas has weddings every day. We can reschedule."

"Like a business meeting," she murmured.

He stroked her cheek. "Ben was sleeping in the old foreman's shack. He may be getting too old to live the life of a gypsy."

"How do you know where he was sleeping?"

"I found him there. I tried to ask him for your hand in marriage, but it wasn't the most encouraging conversation."

An old, painful memory slid forward. "Oh?"

"Yeah. I can't say he exactly gave me his blessing, but I made it clear how much I wanted to marry you. We left it at that."

Laura doubted anything had been *left*. Ben had refused his blessing when Dave had asked him, as well. And now Ben was in the hospital with sudden chest pains. Was a short-term marriage, a year of life with Gabriel, worth going through this again? She should have seen this coming. Ben was uneasy about the Morgans and he definitely wasn't going to give her away to them without a fight. "Was he upset?"

"No more or less than usual. At least he didn't take another shot at me." He turned her chin up so he could look into her eyes. "Ben's illness is not because we plan to get married."

She hated how worried she'd sounded. "I'd like to wait until he's better before we…before we do anything."

"I agree." Gabriel nodded, gently releasing her. "Where are the children?"

"Mimi's looking after them."

"I'll swing by and grab them, if you want. I can keep them while you're here with your father."

She looked at him, her blue eyes a bit guilty. "Are you sure you're ready for that? They can be a handful."

He grinned. "I think I can handle your crew."

He certainly seemed to look forward to the challenge. "I hope you know what you're signing on for."

He shook his head. "I've enlisted before. This will be a piece of cake. Call me if you need anything."

He went off, not the least bit bothered by her hesitation to marry him, not worried about Ben's non-blessing. Dave had been bothered by it, but she had the sudden impression that Gabriel was not the kind of man who would give a damn. He'd love the blessing, but if not, he sure wouldn't lose any sleep over it.

Maybe Ben had a simple case of heartburn, and then none of this would matter. Perhaps Gabriel had misunderstood her father's reticence about their marriage.

She knew Gabriel had misunderstood nothing.

"Mrs. Adams?"

She turned to face a doctor. "Yes?"

"I'm Dr. Carlson. I understand that you're your father's only relative who can see to his care?"

"I am." Chills suddenly ran through her.

"He's had a mild heart attack. Nothing severe, but we're going to keep him here overnight. We're evaluating his condition and need to run some tests. We'll look for a blockage, or other issue that may have caused this."

"Thank you." She felt ashamed for wondering

whether her father had staged a heart attack to keep her from marrying Gabriel. "Can I see him?"

"For a minute. Then I want you to go home and get some rest."

She nodded, following the doctor into her father's hospital room. "How are you doing?"

"I'm fine," Ben said. "These doctors need to let me out of here."

She patted his hand. "Stay calm, Dad. Don't get excited."

He sighed. "I am not a good patient."

She nodded. "Most people aren't. But the doctor says I can only stay a moment."

"Guess I messed up your wedding." He didn't look too unhappy about that. "I told Gabriel I didn't think he deserved you."

"I know. He told me."

Ben twisted his lips. "Guess I worried myself into a little chest pain."

Guilt jumped inside her. "You shouldn't have. I'm a big girl, Dad."

"Fathers worry. That's what we do."

She shook her head. "You need to let go."

He nodded. "I guess it was just a shock. I felt like you and I had just patched things together, and then suddenly I needed to keep you to myself. Felt like I had to fight for you. You know I don't trust those damn Morgans."

"This is my decision, Dad. Gabriel's a good man."

"You say that about Josiah, too, and he's a scoundrel."

She laughed and kissed her father lightly on his forehead. "He's not the only scoundrel in Union Junction."

Ben grunted.

"I'm leaving before your blood pressure skyrockets."

"I think it already did," he said, in a bid to get more attention.

She smiled. "I'll be back tomorrow."

He looked at her, his eyes big and sad. "I wish you could stay my little girl."

She blew him a kiss and backed away, feeling like the worst daughter in the world.

GABRIEL SMILED WHEN MIMI opened the door. "Hello, Mimi."

"Come in, Gabriel. How's the patient?"

He looked around the big, welcoming entry of the house at the Double M ranch. Gabriel could honestly say he wouldn't mind having a place like this one day, where little feet could run and play, and he and Laura could raise their family.

He seemed to think about Laura and the life he wanted with her all the time. "Nice place, by the way."

"Thank you."

"The patient isn't pleased to be a patient," Gabriel said.

"I wouldn't expect Mr. Smith would be happy to be in the hospital." Mimi ushered Gabriel into the kitchen. Through the window, he could see Penny and Perrin playing with Mimi's brood. Though Mimi's children were a bit older, they included Laura's children in their activities. There was a large swing set and fort, a sandbox and a couple of Hoppity Hops littering the lawn.

He remembered having a Hoppity Hop. Jack had been the best of all of them when it came to racing on them; maybe it had been good early training for the rodeo.

Mimi glanced over her shoulder at the children. "They make me smile, too. Laura's done a great job with her kids."

"Yeah." He couldn't wipe the smile from his face.

"So I hear congratulations are in order?"

He dragged his gaze away from the children. "I hope so. When Ben gets well, congratulations will be in order."

Mimi smiled. "Laura sounded happy about marrying you."

That shocked him. If anything, she'd seemed reluctant to him. "Glad to hear it."

"She asked me not to tell anyone what you were planning, but she felt like you two are very comfortable despite only knowing each other a short while. I take it you want a low-key wedding?"

He nodded, not certain what Laura would want if the circumstances were romantic rather than advantageous.

"I know you'd planned for an elopement," Mimi said carefully, "but I also know you were having to plan spur of the moment. So Mason and I were wondering if perhaps—when Ben gets well, of course—if you'd like to get married at the Double M."

He blinked, instantly able to see Laura in a pretty dress on the wide green lawns of the Double M. It was the kind of wedding she deserved. "That's very generous of you and Mason."

Mimi smiled. "It would be our wedding gift to you and Laura. Then Penny and Perrin could be at the wedding, and by then Ben will be well enough to give his daughter away."

Gabriel wasn't sure Ben would be up to the task. Laura would have to be pried out of his grasp.

"You know he didn't get to give her away before."

Gabriel shook his head. "I didn't know that."

"Ben was so dead set against Laura marrying Dave that Laura ended up eloping. Coincidentally, they married in Vegas. She said it wasn't what she'd wanted, but she'd had no choice." Mimi put some biscuits on the counter and covered them with a plaid napkin. She set some fresh fruit out in a bowl, and the washed fruit shone in the light. "Laura may feel differently, and my feelings won't be hurt if you don't take Mason and me up on our offer, but it does seem that a woman should have one hometown wedding in her life. Don't you think?"

He certainly agreed. In fact, he wanted no reminders of Laura's first wedding. "Thank you, Mimi. I'll see if I can budge her on the matter." He wasn't sure what Laura would say. Pieces of the future were fitting together in his mind, and the more he thought about a traditional wedding, with vows spoken in front of family, and Penny and Perrin there, the more he knew he wanted this moment to feel like forever.

He could see wanting Laura for the rest of his life.

Now that his father had returned, and the deal was off, he didn't need a one-year marriage. He didn't need to get married at all. He could go back to being as unattached as he was before.

But that wasn't what he wanted, not his freedom nor a one-year marriage. Suddenly, he was grateful that Ben's heart condition had slowed everything down. Somehow he needed to convince Laura that he had changed—she could trust him for something deeper than a fast fix.

Chapter Twelve

Gabriel drove Penny and Perrin to his house, feeling pretty good about how excited they'd acted to see him. Of course, Perrin didn't show his enthusiasm quite like Penny, but the baby definitely seemed pleased. He'd debated whether to take them to Laura's house where they'd be among familiar things, then decided he'd head over to Josiah's. His father would enjoy seeing the kids—it might even soften the old man up a bit.

Penny and Perrin might be the only way to put a smile on Josiah's face. Penny saw Josiah on the front porch and ran to be enveloped in his arms.

"This is a surprise," Josiah told Gabriel. Josiah's eyes glimmered gratefully at Gabriel. In that moment, Gabriel knew he was going to spend extra energy trying to connect with his father. It could be his father lying in that hospital. As cranky as Josiah was, he didn't want to shortchange their relationship.

"Didn't figure you'd mind," Gabriel said.

"Nope. Come out here, kids. I have something to show you."

The four of them walked to a south paddock. A small white pony stood grazing, glancing up at them before returning her attention to the grass.

"Horse!" Penny exclaimed. "Can I ride her?"

Josiah laughed. "As soon as she gets settled in, you may ride her. Perrin, too, when he's old enough. I bought that pony for you kids."

Gabriel raised a brow at his father. "You bought them a pony?"

"Every child should have a pony. At least every child who wants one, and who has a little land."

Gabriel watched as Penny held out a piece of grass to try to lure the pony to her. "You never bought us a pony."

Josiah grinned. "You boys were too busy rappelling out your bedroom window to need a pony. You got plenty of exercise."

"So you cut that limb off on purpose?"

Josiah nodded. "Just hadn't figured on the rope ladder."

It felt good to talk about the past. The moments of ease that peeked into their relationship felt healing.

"So, how's my thin-skinned farmhand doing?"

Gabriel snorted. "Ben's tough."

"I didn't need you hiring half a man to work this place."

Gabriel looked at his dad. "You weren't supposed to be here. So I made an appropriate hire. The man has plenty of experience. Not to mention that you ran off two able-bodied sons."

"I didn't run them off. They deserted."

"You didn't make them feel welcome." He didn't

feel welcome, either, but he had Penny and Perrin to think of.

"What was I supposed to do? Buy them a pony?" Josiah asked.

"You're supposed to just be nice," Gabriel said. "It gets you what you want. Especially after you've gone to the trouble to gather everybody around."

Josiah grunted.

"You might as well tell me," he said, helping Perrin to put his feet on the bottom of a wood rail, "why you went to the trouble of scheming to get us all home."

His father picked Penny up, kissed her on the cheek. "So did Ben ruin any chance of you and Laura getting married? You know he's pulling this sickly routine on purpose."

"I don't know that to be true."

"Ah, hell, yeah, Ben was probably one of those kids who threw fits."

"Shh, that's their grandfather," Gabriel cautioned.

Josiah shrugged. "It's true. Anyway, here comes Laura. We'll ask her how the hypochondriac is doing."

"I wouldn't phrase it that way," Gabriel said, making Josiah laugh.

"Hi," Gabriel said, when Laura walked to the fence. "How did you know we were here?"

"Where else would you go?" She looked up at him, her eyes dark with fatigue. "This is your home."

True. He didn't glance at his father. "How's Ben?"

"Fine, for the moment," Laura said. "Still, he needs a change in diet and an improved lifestyle. The doctor feels he's under too much stress."

Josiah turned away with Penny in his arms. Gabriel thought he'd seen a grin on Josiah's face. "Glad he's going to be all right."

"Gabriel, can I talk to you?"

"I'll take the kids in for a snack," Josiah offered. "Good news about your father, Laura."

"Thank you." She pushed her hair back, though the early-morning breeze pulled it forward again. "Gabriel, maybe we were moving too quickly."

He watched her intently. Damned if Ben didn't appear to be winning the battle. "Maybe. Maybe not."

Laura looked uncertain. "I don't want to cause my father any stress."

"Of course not." Gabriel shook his head in sympathy.

"Since you and your father appear to be getting along better, you probably don't need my help any longer."

"Your help?"

"By marrying you," Laura said quickly.

"Oh." Her face was so drawn that Gabriel realized it was Laura who was stressed, maybe more than Ben. She was afraid. Afraid that her relationship with her father might be forever on hold if he suddenly died. She was afraid that marrying against her father's wishes a second time might be too much for him to take. "I understand your position."

"Thank you," she said on a rush. "I've got to get back to the hospital."

"Leave the kids here," he said quietly. "Dad and I are enjoying them."

"Dad?" she said. "Not Pop?"

He shook his head. "It doesn't matter. You go on. I'll take good care of the children."

"Thank you so much for understanding."

"Yeah. I'm just that kind of a great guy," he said as she got into her small seen-better-days car. He waved as she drove away, though it was hard to pull off the lightheartedness. The pony neared the fence, eying him curiously. "There went my bride," he told the pony. "She has no idea I want to marry her for real. I've fallen in love with her, and I don't think she sees me quite the same way."

It hurt. And he was pretty sure that a gentleman would back off and be an understanding kind of guy. He could do that, in fact, would do that, since she'd asked it of him, but he recognized it was going to take a chunk of his soul to act like he was good with it.

At least he still had Penny and Perrin. He was pretty sure they liked him. He headed inside to find out.

Penny and Perrin were riding on Josiah like he was an energetic *horsey.* For his part, Josiah seemed to enjoy the game as much as the kids. He neighed, pawed the air and generally acted silly. "I can't remember you doing that for us," Gabriel commented.

Josiah let out a gleeful neigh, his white hair shaking as he pretended to be a horse. "Where do you think I got these skills?"

"I thought Penny and Perrin conned you into being a substitute for the pony you bought them. Does Laura know you did that?"

"We need not share that just yet." Josiah carefully rode Perrin across the "creek," a swath of the den where the furniture had been pushed away. "She was in a bit of a hurry to get back to Ben, wasn't she? Think he's really all right?"

"I guess so." Gabriel went into the kitchen to make tea and grab some of the cookies the church ladies had recently left. The realization that Josiah was in town and bearing gifts had brought many containers of delicious treats to their house. It was too bad Pete and Dane had elected to leave—the eats were fantastic. Gabriel munched on a double chocolate chip cookie from a box labeled Thank You For Everything, Mrs. Gaines.

"What'd you do for Mrs. Gaines?" He set the cookie tray on the table and pulled Perrin into his lap. "No cookies for you, sir. You get something more delicious, like one of these meat stick thingies your mom left you. Ugh. Probably better for you, but still."

"She's the town librarian. They had a wish list last Christmas that asked for a new reference set. Times have changed, you know. Nobody hardly wants the big fat books as much. They want the CD versions, or the Web site subscriptions, and that takes updated technology. I left a little money to cover the technology." He swiped a cookie, set Penny beside him, stuck a napkin in her hand—the picture of a happy grandfather. "It's especially important for the high schoolers who want to study in the library. Not everybody has a computer in their home."

"Yeah, Dad, about that." Gabriel sipped at some iced tea, carefully moving Perrin's hand away from the cookie tray and giving him an animal cracker instead. "I know kids don't always remember everything their parents did for them, but it does seem that you've entered a new, more benevolent stage of your life. One we aren't familiar with."

"You're asking why I didn't coddle you boys since I had so much money. Why I kicked your asses instead of giving out hugs. Why I tried to make men out of you instead of pansy-assed good-for-nothings who were always looking for a handout."

"In so many words," Gabriel said, "I suppose you just gave me the answer."

"Kids who have everything handed to them generally don't fare well. You boys were already a little wild. You had no mother to soften you. I was busy running things and couldn't mother hen you. I figured if you had it in you to be successful, you'd get there on your own. And if you didn't, you'd only have yourself to blame."

Gabriel nodded. "I see your point." He saw it, but that didn't address the affection part of the parenting equation, the pleasure of enjoying your child. "So the reason you're spoiling Penny and Perrin is—"

"I can enjoy being a doting grandfather if I want."

"I can't speak for my brothers, of course, but seeing the softer side of you—"

"I'll tell you something, Gabriel. Since you're being honest, and since you hung around, which frankly shows some of what I was trying to teach you boys sunk in, which is to face the hardest parts of life bravely—I liked watching you kids struggle. I liked seeing you get tough. Raising men is a hard thing. Raising whiners is easy." He kissed Penny on the forehead and handed her another cookie. "But in case you feel left out—and I suspect you do or you wouldn't be trying to improve my parenting skills—I'll tell you a little secret."

"Shoot," Gabriel said dryly. "I'm all ears."

"Now, this is just between you and me—"

"Absolutely," Gabriel said. Who the hell would he tell?

"I put the million dollars that you would have received for staying here one year into a bank draft in your name this morning."

Gabriel looked at his father. "What's the hook?"

Josiah laughed. "There is no hook. You proved yourself. You came here, and you would have stayed. You alone cared enough to try to patch up our differences. I see in you a son I can be proud of."

That meant more to him than the money. "Thank you."

Josiah nodded. "Jack didn't even bother to show up. He doesn't give a damn. He'll still get his chance, but—" Josiah shrugged "—he and the rest of your brothers have to live under the same rules you played by."

"Okay," Gabriel said, "did you come home because you wanted to see us, or was it all just a test?"

Josiah grabbed a red ball, scooted near the fireplace and rolled it to Penny, who rolled it back. He then rolled it to Perrin, who couldn't roll so well, so Gabriel helped him.

"When Laura let me know you had come home, I chose to come home," Josiah said. "It was a test, maybe, but I also wanted very much to see you."

"Laura?" Gabriel frowned.

"Did you think I was psychic?" Josiah grinned.

"Laura had instructions to let me know if any of my sons returned."

Gabriel wondered what else she was keeping to herself. "Guess she did her job."

"I'm leaving in the morning." Josiah stood, his shaggy hair bushing out around his shoulders. "I have to get back to work. It keeps a man alive, you know."

"I hope so." It was all he had right now. "So what are your plans for this place?"

"You're here. You can take care of it. You have the money to do whatever else you like, but I wouldn't tell anyone, if you want to know if they care for you."

Gabriel wondered if that was a veiled reference to Laura, but he didn't think she was fixated on money or she would have said yes to him instead of backing out on him when her father had chest pains.

"There's an account and books for the ranch specifically. I know I can trust you with the running of it."

"Ever thought about selling?"

Josiah shook his head. "Nope. I love my place in France and I'm thinking on buying one in Florida, but this ranch represents what I believe is best about life. Feel free to make it your home as long as you want."

"And if Pete and Dane come back?"

Josiah shrugged and headed up the stairs.

"Jeez," he said to Penny and Perrin. "He's got me stuck right in the middle."

Penny smiled at him. "Morgan," she said, enjoying saying the name.

"That's me," he said, and wondered why he suddenly felt okay with that.

WHEN LAURA CAME TO PICK up the kids that night, Gabriel had a surprise for her. "Chicken on the grill, canned corn and a salad. Not as good as you made me when I first arrived in Union Junction, but as good as I can do. I know you're probably worn out."

"I'm all right." She glanced at the food. Penny and Perrin were seated at the table. Somewhere Gabriel had found a small chair he'd sort of roped Perrin in to; sailor's knots held her son's roundness into the chair. Mashed peas decorated the table in front of Perrin. "It's hard babysitting when you're not used to it."

"It's good practice for me. And Dad's been helping." She slid into the chair. "Thank you. It looks delicious."

"So. This is what we'll look like every night if you keep my proposal in mind." He lit two candles in the center of the table with a flourish. "I'm just saying."

"I can't." Laura shook her head. "Ben is just too upset about it. And I can't go through that again. I'm sorry, Gabriel."

"You have no idea what you're passing up." He'd thought a lot about it, and he wasn't about to let this woman go just because Ben was having a coronary. If anything was killing the man, it was his own bitterness.

Steps sounded on the stairs. Josiah came into the room, his laugh booming when he saw the children at the table. "You two don't need to eat. You need to see a pony!"

"Yay!" Penny jumped up from the table.

"Young lady!" Laura shook her head. "Mr. Morgan, they must excuse themselves."

"All right. Excuse us all," Josiah said, rescuing Perrin

from his sailor's knots. "We have to go walk a pony, and then I need to do some things in town. I'll only be gone a couple of hours, Laura, so don't get jittery. You and Gabriel enjoy the food. He's been cussing at the grill for an hour."

Gabriel nodded. "It's true. I am not the griller that my brothers are."

"Looks like you did a fine job," Josiah said, looking at the meal, "but the kids and I are having ice cream for dinner. Even Perrin can have ice cream instead of those peas, can't he?" he asked, nuzzling the baby as he carried him out. "And I saw my son feed you that nasty meat stick thingie from a jar earlier. If I was you, Perrin, I'd complain. Come on, Penny, honey, you and I will have a swirl with candies on top."

The door closed behind them. Gabriel shook his head. "I didn't even know he knew that there was a roadside ice-cream store that offered swirls with candies on top."

"He's always been this way with my children." Laura seemed resigned to it. "The gifts are getting bigger, however."

He'd just had a huge one tossed into his life. He wasn't sure how to take the fact that he now had a million dollars to his name, free and clear. He didn't even have to live here, didn't have to put up with Josiah, didn't have to take care of Laura.

He was free.

"So, Laura," he said, "I understand you're the little birdie who let Josiah know I was here."

She hesitated as she served them corn. "Yes, I did."

"You weren't going to tell me."

"No. Do you have a problem with that?"

He grinned. "I probably should, but I like that mysterious edge you've got going on." Reaching over, he captured her hand in his. She dropped the spoon into the corn as he pulled her into his lap. "Suddenly, this dinner doesn't seem as inviting as what I've got in my lap right now."

He kissed her, and Laura had no desire to pull away. She knew her father would be so angry—Ben really thought he was looking out for her best interests—but just like before, she was falling for the man and not the approval. Gabriel kissed differently than her husband had and she relished that. She wanted everything about this to be different.

It was important that she never look back. She didn't ever want to feel the same. She wanted this, and more and everything Gabriel wanted to give her—except marriage. She couldn't do that. She knew that now. Ben falling ill had convinced her that she had agreed to marriage for all the wrong reasons. She was agreeing to marry for stability, when all she really wanted was to feel alive again.

Gabriel moved his hand to her waist, and then along her sides to her breasts. Her breath caught. She sensed him waiting, asking permission. Gabriel was a gentleman; he would never override her wishes. But she wanted him, wanted what he was offering her and so she kissed him back, letting her hands move down his chest—and then lower.

His breath hitched, and she knew he wanted her the way she wanted him.

"You're making me crazy," he told her.

"I want to."

"I'm going to drive you crazy, too," he said, "and then make you the happiest woman on earth."

He already was. Her blood steamed in her body, her skin craved his touch. But she feared Josiah and the children would walk in and see them.

Gabriel carried her upstairs, laid her in his bed. Kissed her inch by inch, her entire body, chasing away her fears. Made her know that everything about this moment would be different from anything she'd ever known—and when he finally claimed her, Laura knew she'd never be the same again.

Hunger had been born inside her, and only Gabriel could satisfy it.

"GET OUT OF BED, OLD MAN."

Josiah looked down at his nemesis, allowing his lips to curl. Ben's eyes flew open—then he grinned at Josiah.

"I'm quite comfortable, thank you. Appreciate the visit, though." Ben glanced around. "What brings you? An apology?"

"Hell, no. What would I apologize for?"

"For trying to kill me when you learned I took Gisella to the airport. I was trying to do a neighborly deed, caught between a rock and a hard place was I—"

"Let's not live in the past," Josiah snapped. "Forgiveness isn't one of my more saintly qualities."

"I'll say." Ben shuddered. "They'll not be putting your name forth for beatification no matter how much money you give away."

Josiah sighed. "The kids want to see their sad sack of a grandfather. Right now, they're eating fruit cups in the cafeteria with a nurse friend of mine. You and I have something to discuss."

Ben glared at him. "I'm on my deathbed."

"You're throwing a pity party, and I want it to cease. Or I'll consider myself invited."

Ben wrinkled his face. "You've never been much fun at a party."

Josiah laughed heartily. "Now, listen, old man, you think you're playing me and everyone else like a well-strung fiddle. But you leave Gabriel and Laura alone."

Ben's gaze narrowed. "Why should I? He's trying to marry my daughter, and that just ain't gonna happen."

"Thanks to you, it probably won't."

"I see no reason to mingle my blood with yours, Morgan. It would dilute the purity of my good name."

"Ben, you sorry ass—if you weren't connected to an IV, I'd kick your selfish butt."

Ben shrugged. "And everybody would say look at poor Ben being picked on by that awful Josiah Morgan."

"No, they wouldn't. They'd say poor Josiah Morgan, having to put up with that conniving Ben Smith."

"Damn you!" Ben looked like he wanted to hop out of bed and take a swing at Josiah. "I'm not a conniver! No more so than you, Josiah Morgan!"

"You are if you're lying in this bed making your daughter feel guilty about wanting to be with my son."

"How the hell do you expect me to feel? After you cheated me?"

Josiah grimaced. "I didn't cheat you. You think you put one over on me, and I'm letting you gloat on that, but if you don't give my son your blessing, I'm going to put an end to your game."

Ben looked at him suspiciously. "What are you talking about?"

Josiah tapped him on the arm. "Old friend, I'm talking about that false rumor you put about that there was oil on your property."

Ben blinked. "Don't know what you're talking about."

"Sure you do. You told everyone you thought there might be oil. Then you asked me to buy your land at an inflated price. Then you ran around screaming about how I'd taken advantage of you. I knew there was no oil, I knew there was little value to your land and that you were hard up for cash. What happened to that cash, by the way?" Josiah asked, a gleam in his eyes.

"It's…in a safe." Ben waved a hand. "Anyway, it's none of your business."

"Funny how you're shacking up in my foreman's house if you have the money somewhere. Over a half million dollars, and you don't even buy your grandchildren a trip to the county fair. Yet I hear you going all over town about how I cheated you."

"Probably you did, Josiah. You always get the best of a person."

Josiah's white brows raised. "Did you gamble away that money?"

"No!"

"Did you drink it up?"

"No!"

Josiah leaned close. "Then tell me what happened to it."

Ben sighed. "I put it in a vault in the bank so it couldn't be traced to me for taxes."

Josiah frowned. "You would have had to report the sale of your land."

"That's why I tell everyone you cheated me. So I won't have to pay capital gains."

Josiah wondered if the man truly didn't understand the law. "Do you understand that few people cheat Uncle Sam and get away with it?"

"Do you understand that that is the only time I'll see that much money? Do you know how hard it is to make it as a farmer?" Ben crossed his arms. "I'm not giving one cent of it to the government. I've paid taxes for years. When did the government ever help me?"

Josiah scratched his head. "At the very minimum, when you get caught, you'll have to pay interest on what you owe."

"I'll be dead by then."

Josiah shrugged. "And your estate will still have to pay. I'm not sure what you've done helps Penny and Perrin."

Ben sighed. "It was just hard to give up any of that dough. I wanted money all my life, just a little something in the bank that gave me security. Something I could pass to my daughter without everybody thinking I'd been a failure all my life."

"Don't you think she'd have been just as happy with you being honorable?"

Ben shook his head. "I can take care of her, and my grandkids, without asking anybody for a dime if we ever fall on hard times."

"Laura seems independent to me. Besides, Ben, sleeping in my foreman's shack isn't exactly living the high life."

"It's free. Seems like a bargain to me, and I'm satisfied with that."

Josiah had to admire the man's desire to keep what was his. "But you've just about done in your ticker."

"That's because your son is trying to take my daughter away from me."

"You're just trying to keep her away from me." Josiah sat down near his nemesis. "Be honest and don't juggle facts for a change."

Ben snorted. "I don't completely cotton to Morgans, I'll admit. Some are better than others."

"But is that fair to your grandchildren?" He leaned close to stare Ben down. "Gabriel would do fine by them."

Ben's gaze slid away. "Not sure about that. But if it'll make you quit harping on me, I promise to pay the taxes on the money you paid me for the land."

Josiah sighed. "Don't get me back on that. This entire matter is between you and me, and you need to butt out of Laura's life. You nearly got yourself sidelined for good, you know. Interfering is not healthy."

"Says the greatest interferer I ever met." Ben's eyes closed. "Anyway, you don't even like your own sons. Why should I?"

Josiah shook his head. Ben had it all wrong. He clearly didn't understand the Bible's instruction: *What son is there whom a father does not chasten?* The way he'd raised his sons was the only way to raise good men. But Ben was so stubborn it was hard to move him. Laura probably had some of those stubborn genes in her, which didn't bode well for Gabriel, who was pretty mulish himself.

Josiah wished he could make it all better, but he couldn't. The die had already been cast. He went to get Penny and Perrin to sneak them in to see their grandfather—no kids allowed in this area, especially past visiting hours—but he figured what the hell. He'd given enough money to the hospital to buy beds for a new wing. One day, it might be him lying in one of these beds, and he sure hoped Ben would care enough to sneak the kids in to see him.

Maybe he would, and maybe he wouldn't. Josiah couldn't divine whether forgiveness lay in store for him, from anyone. But life was all about family, and Josiah was doing his damnedest to try to build one.

Chapter Thirteen

The moment he made love to Laura, Gabriel was even more determined to romance her until she couldn't say no to his marriage proposal. But he was aware this wouldn't be easy. He moved her arms above her head, trapping them against the pillows, then languidly licked each nipple. He loved the gasp he pulled from her.

"Gabriel," she murmured, a slight protest, and since he knew she was going to use going to visit her father as an excuse, he slid inside her, keeping her with him for a few more minutes.

"Yes?" he asked.

She moved up against him, welcoming him. "Don't stop."

He laughed. "Are you sure?" He teased her with another slow thrust.

She clutched at him, pulled his head down so that he could kiss her. This closeness with one person was what he'd been missing all his life. He kissed her fast, hard, possessively, and let himself enjoy the feel of her unresisting in his arms.

AN HOUR LATER, LAURA GASPED and jumped from the bed, grabbing at her clothes. "I hear your father's truck!"

"It's all right. It'll take him a minute to get the kids out of their seat belts."

Laura gasped again, jumping into her clothes. "The children can't see me like this! Hurry, Gabriel!"

The joys of parenthood. Gabriel grinned. "That's what you said not an hour ago."

"Don't tease me now," she said. "No mother wants her children to find her naked in bed with a man she's not married to."

"Yes, we should fix that."

She tossed him his shirt. "Some things can't be fixed, you know."

He handed her the tiny black panties that had gotten hung on his belt buckle. "Female undergarments amaze me. Are they utilitarian or just for turning a man on? These certainly seem more sexy than functional. Can't say that's a bad thing."

"Gabriel!" She moved his boots over to him and slipped on her panties and then her sandals. Her fingers flew through her hair as she glanced out the window. "Oh, they're looking at the pony. Why did your father buy a pony when he won't be here long?"

"He bought it for your kids," Gabriel said absently, thinking through the logic of what Laura had just said. He followed her down the stairs. Josiah had said he was leaving in the morning. Why would he have bought a pony that couldn't be ridden yet?

"My kids! Penny and Perrin aren't really old enough to ride. Besides, we're never over here."

"I know." They sat down at the dinner table they'd abandoned two hours ago. The candles were burned down to the sticks and had put themselves out. The food was cold, but Gabriel would have eaten it anyway except for the look on Laura's face. "What?"

"He bought a pony for my children," she repeated. "Obviously he plans on them being around here. With you."

"You'd have to ask Pop about that. I don't really understand him myself. I'm just now learning the whole father-son thing in a new way. It's a whole new language I'm decoding."

"Gabriel!"

"Yes?" He looked at Laura. "Do you know you're beautiful when you're not wearing makeup and your hair is out of place?"

She opened her mouth to say something when Josiah walked in with the kids. He had Penny by the hand and Perrin soundly sleeping tucked up against his chest. "You two still eating?" Josiah asked. "Must be some hungry folk."

He glanced at the plates and saw that they hadn't been touched. "Ah, you know in France and Italy people tend to take longer meals. It's good for the digestion," he said to cover Laura's embarrassment. She could barely look at Josiah.

He handed her Perrin gently. "This one's a snoozer. He was awake for visiting your father, though."

"My father?" Laura looked at Josiah. "You went to see Ben in the hospital?"

"Sure." He put Penny in a chair at the table, glancing at Gabriel like he had something he wanted to say but wouldn't share it in front of Laura. "He's my employee."

Could Ben and Josiah spend five minutes in the same room without a battle breaking out? Gabriel wasn't sure. "So how did that go?"

"He was his usual irascible self, which I attribute to his general well-being." Josiah tucked in to cold corn and chicken. "This is delicious, Gabriel. For a man who lived off of military grub, you seasoned this chicken just right."

"Mr. Morgan," Laura said sternly, "you did not go to pay a social call to Ben."

"I took the grandkids by." Josiah shrugged, his face innocent. "I had some things to say to him. Never know when I might see him again."

Gabriel stared at his father, the pieces falling into place. "Dad," he said, "you gave us a referendum and a game plan, but then you came home in the middle of the playing rules. You gave me money I wasn't expecting. You're gifting the whole town. You bought these kids a pony they're not really old enough to ride and which you will not be here to put them on. You've gone to see your archenemy or rival or whatever you want to call the relationship you've had over the years with Mr. Smith."

Josiah looked at him, his brows furrowed. "So?"

Gabriel glanced at Laura, then at the kids and saw the family setting his father wanted so badly. "A man would have to be knocking on heaven's door to change as much as you are," he said quietly.

Josiah blinked. He didn't reply, confirm, deny.

"Are you sick, Dad?" Gabriel asked.

Josiah shrugged. "Depends upon a man's perception of himself. I happen to think I'm just fine."

"But the doctors don't agree?" Laura asked.

"Now, missy, you just worry about your own father," Josiah said.

Laura shot back, "You're family, too!" which brought an amazing change to Josiah that Gabriel had never seen in all his life.

Tears in Josiah Morgan's eyes.

LAURA WAS SHOCKED BY THE look on Gabriel's face. He looked heartbroken by his father's slight admission of illness. Briefly she wondered how ill Mr. Morgan could truly be—certainly he looked fit. But he wouldn't lean on frailty to get his way, something Ben might do, she conceded unwillingly.

Here at this table sat many of the people she knew as family, and yet one of them had been holding up all the rest of them. "I'm worried about you," she told Mr. Morgan.

"Don't," he said shortly. "Damn doctors don't know what's in God's plan."

"True, but is there something I can do for you?" She glanced at Gabriel, saw that he appreciated her asking the question he apparently could not. Gabriel looked like he'd had his horse shot out from underneath him. He'd made a lucky guess on his father's latest machinations, trying to second-guess him when the truth was much more simple. The man was trying to cobble his family back together.

"No, thank you," Mr. Morgan said, "it's not in my hands."

"Excuse me." Gabriel left the room.

"Now, see, I don't want anybody worrying," Gabriel's father said. "There's too much of life to live without everyone being down."

"He is your son," Laura said gently. "Wouldn't you expect him to be concerned?"

"I'd rather him focus on getting married and having a family. He's traveled around for years," Mr. Morgan said, warming to his subject. "The honest truth is that family is a great thing. I made a lot of mistakes, I know, but family gave me more pleasure in my life than anything else, including making money. Some people would find that shocking."

Laura felt it was best to skip the marriage comments. "I don't think Gabriel getting married will help your health issue."

"Sure it will. That old geezer you call Ben is lying up in a bed because he doesn't want you to marry my son."

Laura sighed. "Mr. Morgan, it's not that easy. And anyway, you can't really say that Ben doesn't know what's best for me when you're busy impressing your will upon your sons, claiming you know what's best for them."

"True," he answered, "but I have to consider my own longevity. And, Laura, won't you please start calling me Josiah?"

Laura refused to allow him off the topic. "You and my father both think that parenting is managing. I'm going to try not to do that with my children." Penny got down from Josiah's lap and went to find her ball. Perrin snoozed comfortably on her shoulder. She loved her children; she could see how she might want to make decisions for them.

"Well, enough of that kind of talk," Josiah said. "I heard there were chocolate chip cookies in the kitchen, so if you'll excuse me, I think I'll brew up some coffee and have a few."

He got up from the table. She watched him walk into the kitchen, big and broad-shouldered. He appeared more robust than Ben, but he wouldn't fake an illness. He wanted to see his sons married more than anything.

She understood that—but it was not something she could help with. Making love with Gabriel had clearly been a mistake. There was no future for them; she knew in her heart she could not go into a second marriage—not now. When they'd planned a temporary marriage, when she'd thought she was helping Gabriel, that had been different. She'd been able to see the beginning and the end of their marriage. Open and shut, like a book. No emotions.

Now it was too complicated. She couldn't see the end, or where the heartache was. She'd barely pulled herself through the abyss this time; she didn't know if she could rescue herself again. The Morgans were unpredictable men. No matter how much she'd fallen for Gabriel, she had to keep herself from the edge, especially for her children's sakes.

Slowly, she stood. "Will you tell Gabriel I said goodbye, Josiah?"

He came out of the kitchen. "Must you leave so soon?"

She knew Gabriel was upset by his father's news. He needed time to think. "I need to get to the hospital early in the morning in case they release Ben."

He nodded. "Let me know if I can help."

She shook her head. "I appreciate everything you've done, Josiah. Everything except the pony."

He grinned. "Every child should ride."

"I'd tell you to quit scheming," she said, "but maybe it's medicinal for you. It's probably keeping you alive."

He roared with laughter, pleased by her outspokenness. But she had a feeling she was right.

GABRIEL WATCHED FROM HIS window as his father said goodbye to Laura and the kids. He saw Josiah kiss each child, saw him laugh at something Laura said before hugging her. Gabriel saw softness and kindness that he'd never experienced from his father, and realized Josiah had reprioritized his life. It wasn't so much Perrin and Penny that had changed his father, though that had something to do with it. Gabriel saw that Josiah had accepted the changes life was pressing upon him. His father was a different man.

He felt sad for all the time that had passed between them, when he had allowed silence to set solid and inflexible between them. After a moment, he pulled out his cell phone.

He hunted around for Dane's number, then made

the call. "Dane," he said. "It's Gabriel. Got a minute? I need to talk."

"Great," Dane said, "I was just about to call you. Have you heard from Pete yet?"

"No." Gabriel watched Laura drive away, saw his father look after the car until it was long gone and then still he stood, eyeing the distance. "What's up?"

"You might want to think about a road trip and be quick about it," Dane said. "Jack took a real ass-stomping in Kearney and this time he's hurt pretty bad."

Chapter Fourteen

As he stared at Jack in intensive care, wired into every machine known to man, Gabriel knew he had to change his whole life. His brother lay very still, his head bandaged, his eyes closed. Pete and Dane had visited first, then Gabriel went in with Josiah. Josiah hadn't had to be dragged to see his son, which surprised Gabriel. In fact, his father had seemed eager to get to Kearney, his fingers drumming anxiously on his knees as Gabriel drove.

Josiah's drawn face hovered over the face of the son he hadn't seen in ten years. Gabriel wanted to push back time. Jack was battered, bruised—almost unrecognizable. "Jack," he whispered, but his brother didn't move. Josiah's shoulders slumped. Slowly, he reached to touch his eldest son's hand, his fingers trembling.

"Has he spoken?" Gabriel asked the nurse, who was changing a bag of IV fluids.

"No. But we know from the cowboys who rode in the ambulance with him that he had a helluva ride before the bull caught him against the rail and dragged him off. His foot caught in a stirrup and he couldn't free it. The clowns did what they could, probably saved his life, according to your brother's friends."

It was the risk that came with rodeo. Gabriel shook his head. They all worked dangerous jobs, and each of them loved their chosen professions. They had the fever to live on the edge. Many times he'd sat shivering in Gdańsk, or baking in San Salvador, wondering why he did what he did.

The answer was easy: The Morgan brothers all did what they did to prove themselves to the old man. And the old man was keeping his own secret of fallibility. *So we're just bashing ourselves on the rocks, trying to get to someplace that doesn't exist.*

"Jack," he murmured again, hoping to see his brother's eyes move. Josiah looked truly distraught. Gabriel wanted to comfort him but he didn't know how. He did know, however, that their father had raised them as he'd thought best as a parent.

Gabriel sighed. The nurse glanced at him. "I'm sorry, we have to keep his visits very short."

"I understand." Gabriel stood, but Josiah lingered at the bedside of his firstborn.

"Come on," Josiah said. "Jack?"

But Jack didn't move. Josiah turned and silently left the room.

"We'll be back tomorrow," Gabriel told the nurse. "Will you call us if there's any change?"

But the only change the next day was that they were told Jack didn't want visitors. Nor the next day. At the end of the week, the family was told that he'd checked himself out. The hospital could give them no further information.

The three remaining brothers and Josiah stood awkwardly in the waiting room digesting the news. Josiah looked as if he'd aged fifteen years. Gabriel watched as Pete and Dane tried to absorb what they'd learned. Finally, they left after giving Josiah an awkward handshake.

Josiah looked at Gabriel. "Was I that bad a parent?"

Gabriel sighed, shaking his head. "We all make mistakes. I've made more than my share." He pulled his stunned father to the sliding doors leading outside. "Come on, Dad. Let's go home."

LAURA HAD JUST PUT THE kids to bed when she heard a knock on the door, an impatient rapping she recognized. She hurried to open the door. "How is your brother?" she asked Gabriel.

"Tough as cowhide." Gabriel reached to grab her, not allowing her to keep an inch between them.

"And your father?" Laura asked breathlessly.

"Equally tough."

His lips searched hers hungrily. "Wait." She pulled away, feeling a new intensity in him. "What happened?"

"Jack disappeared. Crawled off like a wounded animal, I guess. He just went away before any of us ever got to see him conscious."

She gave him a gentle push toward the sofa, which he sank into. "Where are the kids?"

"In bed. Do you want a drink? Food?"

He shook his head. "I'd like to see the kids. I was hoping to catch them before they went to sleep."

As if she'd been listening at the door—and probably she had—Penny came into the room. She crawled up in Gabriel's lap. A warning flashed in Laura's mind. Her daughter was becoming attached to Gabriel, as was she. There was no denying it. Panic spread through her as she recognized a blossoming hope in her chest. She got up to get Perrin out of his crib so they could all be together.

The three of them looked at her with winsome eyes. She knew Gabriel wanted to be with the children; she knew he had to be upset from visiting his brother. "It is a special occasion," she said.

They snuggled up to Gabriel, each child resting against one side of his body. Perrin put his thumb in his mouth, then thought better of it. Penny's eyelids slowly lowered.

"Life is short. Let's make this more than a special occasion," Gabriel said.

Laura looked at him, her senses on alert.

"I want this to be an every night thing," he told her. "You deserve a guy like me, Laura."

She couldn't say no. In spite of her misgivings—and she was scared to death—she couldn't look in those dark eyes and honestly say she didn't want to be his, didn't want him to be a father to her children. "All right," she said, knowing there was no turning back now and not really wanting to anyway.

MIMI WAS DELIGHTED TO help plan a wedding for Laura. She had a friend in a neighboring town who made bridal gowns, so she dragged Laura over to Tulips, Texas, to have her fit in something that "would make Gabriel's mouth water," Mimi said with a flourish. In town, Valentine Jefferson would make her a lovely wedding cake. Mimi assured her no one did them better.

They had Perrin outfitted in a little tuxedo and Penny in a darling flower girl gown. Mimi agreed to serve as the matron of honor. The ladies of the Union Junction salon agreed to do the hair for the wedding, and even trim Gabriel's just a bit. Not enough to take away from the rascal look he had going on, they assured her. They liked his hair growing out of its military cut.

Ben had recovered enough to give Laura away, though he was balking. "Don't know if I should willingly give you to a Morgan," he said, before asking Josiah if he planned on hanging around or hotfooting around the globe. This seemed to annoy Josiah for a minute, before he recovered his good humor at being invited to the wedding.

Pete and Dane sent congratulations. Jack, they never heard from at all. Gabriel was worried, but he knew that his brother was still recovering. He tried not to think about the fact that none of his brothers would be at his wedding, and asked his father to be his best man, an invitation which Josiah readily accepted. His return to France was postponed.

It would have been perfect except that before the rehearsal dinner, Gabriel discovered just how cold his bride's feet actually were. He went by to give Laura the ring he'd bought weeks before and knew by the pink of her nose that she'd been crying.

"You're not having second thoughts?" he asked, remembering how anxious she'd been to marry him before and then how quickly she'd backed away when her father became ill. It was all understandable—but he had to admit to a spur of worry.

She shook her head. "I'm just nervous, I think. You?"

"No way. I'm going to be a husband and a father. Life is good."

She took a deep breath. "Thank you."

"For what?"

"For not being afraid of…stepparenting."

He laid a finger over her lips. "Parenting. No step. When we slow down and you catch your breath, I'd like to adopt Penny and Perrin, if you'll let me."

"I—I have to think about that," she said, wondering why she held back. But the very act of allowing the children to be adopted seemed to push her deceased husband very far into the children's background. Was that the right thing to do?

"There's plenty of time. Right now I'm going to drink a beer with Josiah as my bachelor celebration. I'll see you at the rehearsal tonight." He kissed her goodbye. More than anything, Laura was afraid that she was going to awaken and find this had all been a fairy tale dream just beyond her grasp.

And then she realized why: Gabriel had never told her he loved her. That he was *in* love with her. He loved her children. He really wanted to be a father.

As for love—that word had never crossed Gabriel's lips.

THE REHEARSAL WOULD BE an easy step toward marrying Gabriel. Laura tried to keep calm, telling herself that just because the wedding had grown a little bigger and more elaborate than she'd expected, this was no cause for nerves. Nor was marrying one of the finest men she'd ever met. If she was a little disappointed Gabriel hadn't ever actually said he loved her, she was sure that was something that would come with time.

She reminded herself she was the one who'd insisted on boundaries when he'd first asked her. He was probably trying not to scare her. This time, there was no reason for them to be marrying, except good old-fashioned romance.

The dress she was wearing tonight was a straight column of light silk she'd worn to church many times. Gabriel would never know this gown was old. But her wedding gown was brand-new. Designed by Mimi's friend in Tulip, it was a shell-pink wrapping of silk and lace, falling straight to her ankles without any fuss. She loved the simplicity of it. Nothing about it reminded her of her first wedding, and she felt beautiful when she put it on.

Gabriel would be very handsome in a charcoal-gray tuxedo. She got the kids ready, and headed over to the Morgan ranch. Picnic tables and chairs had been set up on the lawn for the rehearsal dinner. White tents protected the guests from any shower which might fall, but the skies were clear.

She pushed down her rising panic, resenting it. Where were these feelings of worry coming from? Normal bridal nerves, she assured herself. Every bride probably got them.

She hadn't when she'd married Dave.

But she'd been young and idealistic then. Now there were many more people counting on her to make the right decision. The diamond Gabriel had given her sparkled on her finger. It was a bigger diamond than she expected; she'd never dreamed of owning anything so beautiful. Despite the sun, goose pimples ran over her arms.

The minister had asked them to be early, so that he could have a private discussion with Gabriel and Laura. She saw his car parked in the drive so she hurried to knock on the door. It swung open, and Josiah engulfed her in a hug. "You're family now! You don't have to knock on the door like a guest, Laura!"

"Thank you," she said, letting herself enjoy Josiah's bear hug. Across the room, Gabriel smiled at her. The minister smiled at her. It was a happy occasion—nothing to be afraid of.

"I want to go over the solemnity of the vows with you and Gabriel," Pastor Riley said. "This is just some quiet time for us to reflect on the meaning of the ceremony before you say your vows in front of your guests."

"All right." She slid into the chair he held out for her, unable to meet Gabriel's gaze.

"Did either of you want to write any of your own vows?" Pastor Riley asked.

"I don't think so," Laura murmured. They hadn't talked about it—maybe traditional vows were best. Gabriel shook his head.

Nodding, Pastor Riley put on his glasses. "Marriage is a holy occasion, as you know. From the beginning of the vows, which ends with the final instruction, till death do you part—"

Laura stood. Gabriel followed suit, surprised. "I'm sorry. I can't do this. Gabriel, forgive me. I truly thought I was having simple bridal nerves. But it's more than that." She took a deep breath, struggled for the right words. "This feels like a test I know I'm not going to pass."

"Laura," Gabriel said, his tone sympathetic, "would a few moments alone with Pastor Riley help?"

She shook her head, alarmed by the panic spreading inside her. They couldn't possibly understand. She'd done the death-do-you-part thing once. Death did part her from her beloved, cruelly early, and she'd never be able to say those words again knowing how sinister they were. They weren't romantic at all.

"I'm sorry," she repeated. She handed Gabriel the ring and backed away from the table. "I—maybe it's just too soon," she said.

Gabriel followed her. "Laura. Are you all right?"

She gathered up Penny and Perrin, walking them to the car. She strapped the children into their seats. "I can't do it. I suppose in retrospect I wanted a Vegas drive-through type of wedding so it wouldn't seem so momentous. I realize that now. I'm just too scared to get married again, Gabriel. Which sounds silly, I know, but it's not like falling off a bicycle. As Pastor Riley said, the vows are solemn and meaningful—but they don't always last."

"All right. Don't worry. Somehow we'll get this to work out."

"I don't want you to think I'm crazy," she said, trying not to cry.

"No crazier than anybody else around here. Frankly, if we got to the altar without a couple of misfires, we probably wouldn't be doing ourselves any good. Practice makes perfect."

"Do you mean it?" Laura wasn't sure she deserved this much forgiveness.

"Oh, hell yeah." He shrugged. "Go home. Change your clothes. Forget about this whole thing. Call me when…when you can."

She nodded. "Thank you."

He shrugged. "Bye, Penny. Bye, Perrin."

They looked at him through the window and Laura turned on the car and drove away, feeling like she'd just given up the best thing that could have ever happened to her.

"I am so, so sorry," she murmured to the children. "You have no idea what your mother just took from your life."

She had taken the coward's way out, and now she knew she was in love with Gabriel Morgan. And the thought of losing him, the way she had Dave, was a fear she could not face.

"WHAT THE HELL JUST HAPPENED?" Josiah demanded. Pastor Riley looked at Gabriel sympathetically.

Gabriel shrugged. He appreciated the concern, but he really wasn't surprised. "My bride got the jitters."

"Huh." Josiah shook his head. "Laura's always been a cool, practical kind of girl. Usually knows what she wants."

"Oh, she knows what she wants. She just can't figure

out how to get there." Gabriel ushered the minister into the kitchen and poured them all some tea. "I bet wedding cake freezes just fine. Tuxes can be reordered. Pastor, you can use the flowers for this weekend's services, can't you?"

"Or I can have them delivered to some older folks' homes. They'd really appreciate that, Gabriel." Pastor Riley shook his head. "I've known Laura Adams a long time. She's a wonderful woman. She'll come around."

"I know. She's just not a marrying kind of girl. At least not right now," Gabriel replied.

"You know, I think you have a point," Josiah said. "The best things in life don't come easy."

"See? All those good lessons you gave us growing up are coming in handy now," Gabriel said wryly. "A lesser man might give up on a good thing if he hadn't learned that patience is a virtue."

Josiah grunted. "You didn't learn patience in my house."

"That was the military. You taught me life wasn't always easy. I can wait on Laura."

Pastor Riley nodded. "I'll notify Mimi, and she can help me let the guests know. I'm always available when Laura is ready."

"Thanks." He walked Pastor Riley to the door, then headed upstairs. Grabbing a duffel bag, he tossed in shirts, jeans, all his clothing. His father stood in the doorway, watching.

"What are you doing now?"

Gabriel wasn't sure how to explain his plan. "For now, leaving Ben with the upkeep of the ranch."

"I thought you said you were okay with Laura having second thoughts."

Gabriel looked at his father. "She says it's the ceremony she can't go through again. I think she was fine up until the 'I do forever' part." He shrugged. "Luckily for her, I learned life could be very short in the military. If she doesn't want to put the words on it right now, I understand. But I'm still going to be with her, as a husband, and as a father to her children."

Josiah handed him his boots. "And what if she says—"

"She won't," Gabriel said. He'd held that woman, made love to her. He knew how she felt about him. "It's up to me to give her space."

"By moving in with her?"

"By going slow." Gabriel picked up his duffel and shook his father's hand. "When are you leaving for France?"

Josiah grunted. "I was leaving after we threw the paper hearts at the happy couple."

Gabriel grinned. "Plan on making a return trip in the near future."

He walked away, confident that Laura and he could pass whatever test she was worried about—together. She just needed a teacher to help her study, and he had lots of lessons left to give her.

And a wedding ring.

Chapter Fifteen

"I'm so sorry, Mimi, about all your hard work." Knowing that guests needed to be notified, Laura had driven from Gabriel's ranch straight to the Double M. "I just couldn't make myself do it. It was like there was a giant sign that said Go The Other Way flashing at me."

"Well, you're not exactly a runaway bride," Mimi said, hugging her. "You told Gabriel what was happening, and he understood. Believe me, there are a lot of couples in this town who didn't make it to the altar smoothly, and I'm one of them."

Laura couldn't imagine Mason and Mimi not having an easy courtship, but she did remember rumors that Mason had jumped through a few complicated hoops to win Mimi. "Thank you."

"I bet Josiah just about cried." Mimi smiled. "He's been itching to get his boys to the altar."

Laura didn't feel good about that. Josiah had been so good to her and she felt she'd let him down. "I left so quickly I barely saw Josiah. But he'd been so nice, even telling me not to knock on the door anymore now that I was family."

Mimi patted her hand. "You're still family. Josiah made that clear a long time ago."

She felt better. Slowly but surely, her panic ebbed away.

"You did the right thing," Mimi said. "It's never good to feel pushed toward a decision."

"I really do like Gabriel."

Mimi smiled. "I know."

Laura hoped she hadn't lost any chance she'd had with him. He was gorgeous, sexy, kind. Loving. She was in love with him. "I think I was a little nervous that he hasn't told me he loved me."

Mimi paused in the wrapping up of some hors d'oeuvres that had been meant for the rehearsal dinner. "He hasn't?"

Laura shook her head.

"Men don't always talk about their emotions. Sometimes they expect us to divine their feelings."

"I'm not good with divining," Laura said, and Mimi laughed.

"I can't remember how long it took for Mason to tell me he loved me, but it does seem like forever. It was like pulling a mule out of a barn in winter." She put some food into the refrigerator. "Gabriel seems a lot like Mason. You can read a lot about their feelings from their actions."

Gabriel was a man of action. She could count on him to never be boring. "Can I help you with anything?"

Mimi shook her head. "Right now, I want you to go home and put your feet up. Play with your children. Do something relaxing. You've been through a lot lately. Take some time to smell the roses, as they say."

Laura gathered up her children and embraced her friend. Mimi held her for a good long hug, and Laura thought for the hundredth time how lucky she was to have such wonderful people around her.

She drove home, realizing she'd expected Gabriel to be parked in her driveway. He walked over to help her take the kids out of the car. "I hope you know how glad I am to see you," she told him.

He nodded, grinned at her. Desire melted through her, right down to her bones. "I know you want me."

She shook her head and helped Penny to the house; Gabriel carried Perrin. "I wonder why you still want *me*."

"Because I do. That's all I know," Gabriel said, putting Perrin on the floor with his toys. "I'm moving in, unless you object."

"I was hoping you would," Laura said, surprising herself.

"And what about gossip?" he asked.

"I'll try to save your reputation eventually," she said.

He slid her ring across the kitchen table. "Put that in your jewelry box until you're ready for it."

She picked up the beautiful sparkling ring, then handed it back to him with a shake of her head. "Thank you for trying to be a hero. It hasn't gone unnoticed."

He shrugged and got down on the floor with Perrin. Penny came to sit beside him. "I'm going to like this parenting stuff."

GABRIEL TOLD HIMSELF he was doing the right thing. Even if Laura looked nervous, she hadn't kicked him out.

He decided the best path was to start off as friends.

It was going to be hard, but he vowed to go slow. Let her make all the moves. The prize would be worth it in the end.

A persistent ringing of the doorbell sounded. He glanced around for Laura, but she'd gone to the back of the house. Shrugging, he decided that since this was now his home, he could open the door just as well.

Dane and Pete grinned at him. "Hey. You're not supposed to see the bride before the wedding," Pete said. He came inside the house, looking around with approval. "Small. Clean. Bright. I like it."

"The wedding is canceled. Sorry you made the trip." Gabriel looked his brothers over. "You look like just fell out of a laundry bag."

"We've been doing something I never thought I'd do," Dane said. "We volunteered as clowns at a rodeo. Then made a side trip. Can we sit down or not?"

"It's not really my house," Gabriel said, then remembered he was practicing fathering and marriage. "Sure, have a seat. Play with my kids."

Pete eyed him as he sat. "How are they yours if the wedding is canceled? Sorry about that, by the way."

"Don't be. Some things turn out for the best."

"Always the optimist. Did you get cold feet?" Dane shook his head. "Marriage and Morgans don't mix well."

"Laura had second thoughts. So I decided to move in and show her what she's missing out on."

"Brave. Egotistical, but brave." Dane grinned. "I

decided that while I was in town for your nuptials, I'd best take a look at this Miss Suzy Winterstone."

"And?" Gabriel pulled Perrin in to his lap.

"I'm so glad I didn't allow Pop to guilt me into anything. She isn't my type."

"How do you know? Did you talk to her?"

"I watched her playing at the playground with her twins." He glanced at Penny and Perrin. "I'm not cut out for the playground lifestyle. I'm not even cut out for living in Texas."

"You live in Watauga, you're a Texas Ranger," Gabriel reminded him for the hundredth time. "I've never understood you being something you didn't want to be."

"What, like a housemate instead of a husband?" Dane asked, taking a small dig at Gabriel's circumstances. "Jeez, Gabriel, take it easy on a guy. Part of my issue is that I let Pop kick me into the military. I got out as fast as I could, but what else was I suited for besides protecting, keeping order and handling guns?"

"Sounds like an excellent résumé to me," Gabriel said dryly. "So back to the playful Miss Winterstone."

"Okay. She's cute, I have to admit, but a little fuller-figured than I like."

"Because she has year-old twins."

"Perhaps. But I sense she's just one of those big-boned girls."

"Not a bad thing, in my book." Laura was nice and petite, but nobody would call her thin. She had lots of curves he'd love to discover all over again.

"I think she might be German or French or something." Dane shook his head. "If I'd had your skills, I could have probably understood what she was saying to her children."

"Yeah." Gabriel grinned. It sounded as if his brother had happened upon the babysitter at work, but he wasn't going to share that. Let Dane figure it all out on his own—it was more fun that way. "So where are you headed now?"

"Well, since there'll be no wedding, I guess I'm free for the weekend. What's Pop doing?"

"Last I heard, he was heading out."

"And you're staying here?"

"Nothing's moving me," Gabriel said. "This is my family now."

"Wow." Pete shook his head, walked to the door. "You actually already seem like an old married man. Congratulations."

"Thanks." He hated to ask but made himself do it. "Ever hear from Jack?"

"Nah. He went off to lick his wounds. We'll probably never know what happened, you know?" Pete said.

Pete and Dane seemed resigned to this, but it bothered Gabriel. Their family was so sporadic, unsettled. "Keep in touch, all right?"

"I will." Dane waved at him. "Give my regards to the family."

"Why? Aren't you stopping by to see Josiah?"

Dane shook his head. "I've been thinking about that million dollars Pop promised us if we lived in the house for one year."

"Oh, yeah?" Gabriel kept his face blank. "What about it?"

"Do you think he ever meant to give us any money? Or was he just playing a game? Not that it matters, as far as the money goes. I just resent being jerked around by Pop. Don't think I can forgive that."

Gabriel thought about the money that was already in his bank account. His father had sworn him to secrecy, and he figured Josiah knew something about what he was doing. "Can't say, myself."

"You're not going to live there, though."

"Laura wants her children to stay here where they can keep some stability in their life."

"Doesn't bother you to live where her husband lived?" Pete asked.

Gabriel paused. "Can't say it's going to bother me." Pop was right; some things were better left unsaid.

"Sorry. Shouldn't have opened my big fat mouth."

"Don't worry about it. I'm not." He waved goodbye to his brothers and closed the door. Home was where the heart was; he knew that from spending too much time in dangerous places hungering for the promise of home. Penny and Perrin and Laura belonged here. Hopefully he did, too.

"Who was that?" Laura asked, coming into the room. She was freshly showered, her face glowing. He loved seeing her completely natural; he loved being with her in her home.

"Nobody but trouble," he said.

WHEN THE DOORBELL RANG an hour later, Gabriel half expected to see another wedding guest who hadn't yet received the news about the postponement—he refused to say *cancellation*. He and Laura were simply delaying the inevitable.

It was Ben standing on the porch, looking like he'd rather be anywhere but his own daughter's house. "Hi," he said, walking inside. "Can I talk to you, Gabriel?"

"Sure." Why the hell not? Apparently it was his day for surprise visitors, misery loves company for the jilted groom. He motioned Laura's father over to where he'd been sitting with the children.

"Hi, Dad," she said. She walked into the room with her kids. "We're going outside to play in the new sandbox now that it's all put together."

"You do that," Ben said. "I need to talk to Gabriel for a moment."

"Oh? About what?" Laura asked.

"Now don't you worry about that." He kissed his daughter on the forehead. "Sorry about the wedding, but I do understand. Perhaps it's a wee bit soon."

Her glance slid to Gabriel. "I think so."

"Have fun," he told her.

She managed a tentative smile for Gabriel and closed the door behind them.

Ben wasted no time getting to his topic. "Gabriel, I'm sorry as hell the wedding didn't go off like you wanted."

Gabriel looked at Ben, not completely certain he was being truthful.

"But I hear from your father that you're planning on moving in here with my daughter. I have to be honest with you, I don't think that's a good idea."

"Because?"

"Son, you're rushing things. The girl is still grieving for her husband. Not that he was any great favorite of mine, as you know, but I know Laura, and she's a one-man woman."

That didn't make him feel better. "She didn't seem unhappy to have me here."

"See, that's the problem. Laura doesn't know what she wants. Ever since Laura was a baby, she's known exactly what she wanted and had no trouble speaking up about it. This is why I think you're making a terrible mistake."

Gabriel looked at the man he'd known could be both slippery and untrustworthy. "Why would you try to help me?"

"Because of Perrin and Penny," he said simply. "I knew Laura wasn't ready to get married. I believe I tried to steer you away from that."

That's not exactly what he would have called it, but whatever. "I think it's just marriage she was saying no to, not me."

"Well, it's all wrapped up together." Ben raised his hand and waved it airily. "It's all pressure."

Gabriel considered that. "I can see your point."

"I know you want to be here, understand that you want to make a family with my daughter. Truth is, you haven't even taken care of your own house, son. And now you're staking a claim on Laura, when maybe you should be giving her some breathing room."

"I'll take it under advisement." Gabriel didn't like anything he was hearing. He wasn't certain he could trust Ben.

What worried him was wondering if Laura would ever trust him, and want him despite her fears. A cramp hit his gut. He wanted to be here with Penny and Perrin; in fact, he wanted an even bigger family with Laura.

But her father knew her best, and he believed Laura wasn't ready for marriage.

He saw Ben out, then considered his options. Tonight he was going to spend time with the family he wanted. Later, he'd figure out whether his father-in-law-to-be dispensed helpful advice or not.

From the kitchen window he could see Laura and her kids building a small sand castle. It wasn't as grand as the knight's castle Josiah had purchased in France, but big or small, everyone wanted their own castle. He wanted sand castles and Little League and high school proms in his kids' lives. It did his heart good to see Laura enjoying her family. If he was very lucky, maybe one day they would have a child together.

A child seemed like a faraway dream right now. He went into the kitchen and grabbed some hamburger to make patties, veggies for a salad, a little fruit for a child-friendly dessert. He set the table for four and brewed up fresh tea.

Laura smiled when she came inside. She was tousled from playing with Penny and Perrin, and he liked seeing the happiness in her eyes. "You're making dinner?"

"I'm at your service. What time does the family normally eat?"

"This crowd likes to be at the table by six. We eat, then play, maybe watch a video for thirty minutes, have our bath and they go right to bed." Laura seemed uncertain about how much he could stand of kid play. "Feel free to skip the Little Bear video if you want."

He shrugged. "It all sounds great."

She smiled. "I'm going to wash the children up. We hosed off outside but we're still a wee bit sandy."

He wanted to help with that but Ben's words held him back. He hated that he felt he had to retrench his emotions; he felt more like a visitor than a part of the family.

Whether he liked it or not, that was exactly what he was, until Laura said *yes*. Said *I do* with enthusiasm and true joy.

When Laura came back to the table, she sensed a subtle change in Gabriel. He'd gone from being upbeat to quiet. This was supposed to be their rehearsal dinner night, and here he sat eating burgers and watching Little Bear.

She didn't want to lose him. He could have had his choice of women, but he'd picked her and her brood. "I'm sorry about tonight, Gabriel. And the wedding."

"Don't be. Everything works out for the best usually."

But she sensed a lack of conviction in his words, as if he was repeating them simply to reassure himself.

Chapter Sixteen

Gabriel had finally figured out his father. Money wasn't everything to Josiah, though he'd kept a penny-pincher's handle on every cent until lately. Josiah had given Gabriel his portion of the one-year money because he had made an honest effort to rebuild the relationship with his father. Family was more important to Josiah than money.

Gabriel wanted family, too. This family he was watching play on the floor after dinner. He wanted Laura to want him as much as he wanted her. Ben's words rang true to him now. Maybe he'd never be certain of Ben's motivation, but staying here wasn't the way to find out if Laura would ever want him the way he hoped she would.

He stood. Penny and Perrin looked up. Laura looked at him, too. This was going to break his heart, but in the end, it had to be Laura who felt sure of what she could handle in life. "I'm going to head to the ranch."

She hesitated. "I thought you were staying here."

He nodded. "I had planned on it, but I accomplished

what I came here for. We shared our evening together. I don't need a rehearsal to know how much I want to marry you, but I did want to be with you and the children tonight." Gently, he ran a palm over her cheek. "I'll show myself out."

She followed him to the door. "I don't know what to say right now. I think I understand how you feel, but part of me isn't sure."

He smiled. "It'll all get straightened out in time."

He leaned down and kissed her lightly on the lips. "Be seeing you," he said, and went to his truck.

Leaving didn't feel good, but it did feel like the only right thing to do. His heart heavy, knowing now the agony his father had felt wondering if his boys would ever come home, Gabriel drove toward the Morgan ranch.

"WELL," LAURA SAID TO her children, "let's pick up these toys. Maybe we should crawl in my bed together and watch a movie."

The children were silent, helping their mother tidy up. Perrin didn't really help but he picked up a block and handed it to his mother. Penny industriously put the toys in the toy box before turning to look at her mother. "Where is Morgan?"

"He's gone to his house, sweetie," Laura said, before realizing what her daughter called Gabriel. She had always called him Morgan—but Laura knew he wanted to be called *Dad.* He'd gone from calling his father *Pop* to *Dad,* a subtle but noticeable shift in their relationship. She liked that Gabriel was stubborn; he hung on to a situation, no matter how unpleasant or awkward, until he had the right answer. He had commitment bred into his soul.

She knew he would always be there for her and her children.

The only thing holding her back was the fear of the unknown.

"PERFECTLY NORMAL," VALENTINE Jefferson said the next day when Laura went to thank her for the lovely wedding cake, which had ended up in the freezer. "My path to the altar with Crockett was definitely not easy."

"It's a lovely cake." Laura smiled. "Thank you for everything."

Valentine smiled. "Believe it or not, you'll probably appreciate Gabriel more now that you've been through this."

Laura left the shop and went to visit the girls at the Union Junction salon to apologize for taking a day out of their appointments for a wedding that didn't happen.

"Love is a wonderful thing," Delilah said. The head hairstylist had married her truck-driver beau, Jerry, and all had been right in her world ever since. "It just takes time and understanding. You'll know."

Laura shook her head. "I hope so. I thought I was ready—I just didn't realize I wasn't."

"You have a lot to fit into your life." Delilah sat her down, pulled her hair into a ponytail, pressed it into some pretty curls. "Where's my little Penny and Perrin? Perrin should be just about ready for his first haircut."

Laura shook her head. "Gabriel came by and got them this morning. He said he wanted to get to know them, and that it was a day without Mom. He wanted me to have some time to myself. I have a suspicion that he wanted to get them on the new pony Josiah bought and didn't want me around worrying."

Delilah smiled. "He sure does like those kids of yours."

"They like him, too." The knowledge gave her a sense of comfort.

"And your father?"

"Ben hasn't said much lately," Laura said. "It's odd for him, because he had plenty to say about Dave, and about Gabriel, too, at first. Once Dad turned over a new leaf, he seems to be determined to stay in everyone's good graces."

"I've seen people change for the better that I never thought would," Delilah said. "My sister and I battled for years, but once Marvella decided to make positive decisions in her life, she's been a completely different person. She's a joy to be around."

Laura thought about Delilah's words for a long time after she left the salon. Then she realized that everybody around her was making changes in their lives—everyone except her. It was as if she were stuck, rooted to one spot, wanting everything in her world to stay completely still and unmoving. She would always love Dave; he was the father of her children. But what she felt for Gabriel was more mature, more balanced. She didn't need to be ashamed of her feelings or feel obligated to Dave's memory. He'd always hold a special place in her heart.

As Gabriel did now. The place he had in her heart felt warmed, and loved.

She went home to her house. Hesitating only a moment, she went and pulled out the family photo album, wistfully opening it.

The first pages showed photos of her and Dave on various dates: at the movies, snuggling on the sofa, hanging out with friends. A few wedding pictures followed, both of them smiling with happiness. There were many photos from when the children were born; she'd forgotten how snap-happy Dave had been. He'd spent hours compiling photos in an orderly fashion that chronicled pregnancies, first steps, first teeth. Tears of happiness and sadness jumped bittersweet to her eyes. The last photo was of Dave, taken by Laura, of him holding both the children. When he learned he had a life-threatening disease, he said he wanted a photo of him and the children so they would always remember what he looked when he'd been strong and fit. He wanted them to know he'd loved them.

She closed the album and cried one last time for the innocence of her marriage and the good friend she'd lost.

But Dave would know she had loved him, grieved for him and he'd also want her to move on with a good life for their children. He would not want her making a silent shrine to his memory. The husband, the father in the album he had put together, was the man he'd wanted remembered.

She drove to the Morgan ranch, smiling when she saw Penny on top of the white pony. Perrin was held securely in Gabriel's arm as he walked the pony by halter. Each child wore a cowboy hat. Nearby, Ben took pictures, grinning as he recorded his grandchildren's first ride for posterity.

Ben was a changed man, no doubt about that.

She got out of her car and walked to the fence. "Hey, cowboy," she called.

"Hey," Gabriel said, "you made it in time for the big event."

"What's the pony's name?"

"Sugar." Gabriel grinned proudly. "Penny says she's white as sugar. I figured snow was the obvious choice, but she surprised me."

Laura smiled. "Hi, Dad."

Ben held up the camera. "Step inside the paddock and let me snap a photo." He seemed to consider his words. "A family photo."

Laura ducked under the fence and went to stand beside Penny. Gabriel held Perrin and stood stiffly next to Laura.

"Closer," Ben said with a wave of his hand. "I can't fit everything into the picture."

Gabriel and Laura moved slightly together.

"Closer," Ben instructed. "It's hard to get everybody in the shot 'cause Penny's on the pony."

They moved together again. Laura was pretty sure they were close enough for the smallest camera in the world.

"Closer!" Ben examined the picture he'd just taken. "Gabriel, you have to—"

Laura tugged Gabriel's face toward hers and gave him a meaningful kiss. "Close enough?" she asked her father.

"That one's a keeper," Ben replied.

Gabriel looked down at her, his gaze questioning. "Am I getting a message here?"

"I don't know. How are your code-breaking skills?"

"They were always pretty good." Gabriel grinned. "Try me again to make certain I got the right information."

She kissed him, and he held her tightly against him, despite Perrin's attempt to squiggle free and Penny's giggling behind them.

Gabriel's eyes warmed. "That code was easy to decipher."

She took a deep breath. "After everything I've put you through, do you still want to marry me, Gabriel?"

"You're worth the wait," Gabriel said huskily. "You're talking to a man who waited ten years to be a son. I would have waited forever for you. Fortunately, you come around more easily than I do."

"Dad, hand me that camera, please," Laura said. "And if you don't mind, go stand next to the kids and your future son-in-law."

Ben hopped over the fence and stood next to Gabriel, smiling proudly. Laura clicked the camera, then checked the photo. Everyone was smiling and happy. Tears of happiness jumped into her eyes. She would treasure this picture of her new family for always.

Gabriel helped Penny down from the pony. "There'll be steaks and potatoes tonight for dinner," Gabriel said as they walked toward the house. "Stay and eat with us, Ben."

"I'm going to put Sugar up and bed down for the night." Ben grinned at his daughter. "Think I'm going to try to talk my boss into a new bed and maybe some sheets and blankets for the foreman's house. That plaid stuff is old as the hills, and I'm developing a taste for the finer things in life."

Gabriel snorted. "Get what you need, Ben. The cottage needs an update and you might as well make it yours for as long as you want it."

Smiling, Laura took the children upstairs to wash up. Gabriel looked at Ben. "Are you good with me marrying your daughter now?"

Ben gave him a toothy grin. "She came here on her own, didn't she?"

Laura had, indeed, surprising him. She didn't seem so spooked anymore; instead, she radiated calm and happiness. "Yeah. She did."

"I told you you'd be happier if you waited. Good thing you listened to me. Does no good to rush a woman."

"So, Ben," Gabriel said, "there's one thing I have to know. Did you pull a fast one on my father about oil on your property?"

Ben gave him a coy look. "No one pulls a fast one on Josiah Morgan."

He left, and as he walked to his truck, Gabriel saw the old man jump up into the air and kick his heels. He was celebrating, and Gabriel felt like doing the same.

"Hey," Laura said, as she put her children on the floor, "what can I help with?"

He took her into his arms. "Teaching me how to be a good father and husband."

She smiled up into his eyes. "I think you're already

on your way. In fact, I was thinking that maybe it's time for me to give you something you say you want. Weddings are a good time for new beginnings of all kinds, right?"

"Definitely. What am I getting?" he asked, playfully picking her up.

"I was thinking adopting Penny and Perry might make you the—"

"Luckiest man in the world?" He kissed her with gratitude and joy. "I've waited a long time for this moment, and it feels even better than I imagined it would."

Happiness shone in his eyes, and Laura was glad she could bring him joy.

"Home really is where the heart is," Gabriel said, his voice catching. He kissed her again, taking his time to show her how much he cared for her. "I'm in love with you, little mama. I liked you the minute you stood on my porch with chicken and peas."

Hearing Gabriel say he loved her was a pleasure Laura hadn't expected again in her life. "I fell in love with you when I realized you loved my kids like your very own." There was a time she might not have wanted that, but now she knew how blessed her family was to have Gabriel's love.

"I used to think I didn't want kids," he said. "Good thing I'm not stubborn or anything."

She smiled. "Penny and Perrin will try your patience. Be forewarned."

He laughed. "I waited out their mom. I'm a very patient man."

He kissed her, long and sweet, and Laura knew she would always be safe with Gabriel. But even more important, she knew they would always be a family.

Epilogue

This time Gabriel and Laura's wedding went off without a hitch. They married two weeks later on a beautiful cloudless day, and invited everyone in Union Junction who wanted to come celebrate with them. Laura said they'd just needed time to work the kinks out of things, and Gabriel said he was going to keep her busy working kinks out of him for the next fifty years so waiting two weeks hadn't killed him. But happily he'd slid her engagement ring back on her finger, a sweet reclaiming of the woman he loved.

Gabriel thought Laura was the most beautiful bride he'd ever seen. She made him hungry for her just walking around in her shell-pink wedding gown, holding Perrin and keeping a sweetly-dressed Penny at her side. His mind took rapid-fire pictures of his new family, putting them in a mental photo album he would always treasure. Perrin never had colic anymore, and Penny was becoming quite the little pony rider, all positive changes for which Gabriel felt some proud dad ownership.

Ben gave his daughter away willingly. Josiah grinned, a proud best man, his face alight with joy. His approval meant everything to Gabriel, and just seeing his father's happiness healed the old emotional scars for good.

Pete and Dane made it to the wedding this time to serve as groomsmen, and though they never heard from Jack, Gabriel figured his brother's well wishes were with him. Peace was coming over the family, and it felt good to Gabriel. They had a long way to go in the Morgan clan before all the old wounds were healed. Dane and Pete were having a harder time with forgiveness than Gabriel, but the Morgans were getting closer to harmony than they'd been in a decade.

"You've made me a happy man," he told Laura, pulling her to him for a kiss. "Have I told you yet that I love you? Because if I haven't, I'm happy to tell you that I love you, Mrs. Morgan."

Laura laughed. "Not that I'll ever get tired of hearing it, but you have said it a few times in the last hour."

Gabriel grinned at his bride. "When Pastor Riley said I could kiss the bride, I wanted to grab you and never let you go."

Laura smiled at her handsome husband. "*Did* you let go of me willingly? I thought your father tapped you on the shoulder to remind you our wedding guests were waiting for some wedding cake and dancing."

"Remember the kissing booth?" He ran a hand down her back, giving her a gentle hug. "I wanted to beat all those guys away from you. I figured today they can just sit and suffer watching me romance my bride. They'll never get another kiss from you."

She gave him a teasing smile. "Mason lets Mimi volunteer at the kissing booth."

"That's Mason," he said. His eyes held a possessive gleam that made Laura shiver with delight. "I'm a Morgan, and we have never been ones to play well with others."

"We play well together," Laura said. "I love you just the way you are." Their children snuggled close, and Gabriel wrapped them all into his embrace. For Gabriel, this was heaven, his very own Texas lullaby come true.

* * * * *

The Morgan Men will Return!
Watch for Tina Leonard's stories
about Dane, Pete and Jack
in early 2009, only from
Harlequin American Romance.

And now, turn the page for a sneak peek at the next book in THE STATE OF PARENTHOOD *miniseries, Lynnette Kent's SMOKY MOUNTAIN REUNION, coming July 2008.*
Nola Shannon is coming home to the mountains of North Carolina to teach at the private school where she grew up. She's not expecting to meet Mason Reed—her former teacher and former crush— and discover that he's a single father.

"Ms. Shannon?" the voice came from the driver's seat, weaving its way into Nola's dreams. "Ms. Shannon? We've arrived."

Nola blinked, then pried apart her scratchy eyelids. "Thank you." Just as her blurred vision cleared, the car passed through the wrought-iron gates of the Hawkridge School. She had, indeed, arrived.

Then she glance at her watch. Her appointment with her new boss, headmistress of the Hawkridge School, was scheduled for twenty minutes from now. Immediately afterward, she'd be attending her first faculty meeting, which meant being introduced to the other teachers and staff.

That prospect jolted Nola wide awake. With a Ph.D. of her own and a tenure-track position at an Ivy League university, she had no qualms about her professional status. She was doing the Hawkridge School a favor, actually, replacing a teacher who'd taken emergency maternity leave.

But coming back meant facing…well, the past.

She'd spent three years as a student in Hawkridge. She would see what had changed since she left, and what had not. Did the kitchen still make those delectable yeast rolls for dinner every night? Had the tennis courts been resurfaced, had the dorm rooms been painted? Would she feel at home there, as she once had, or like an intruder from another world?

Nola realized her hands were shaking. She gripped them together in her lap and stared out the window, trying to divert her thoughts with the scenery. All along the winding mountain road, white dogwood flowers fluttered around the tall pine tree trunks. Patches of purple rhododendron blossoms brightened the dappled shade. Some long-dead gardener had planted drifts of daffodils in the grass at the edge of the forest, and their cheerful yellow trumpets nodded in the breeze. As a teenager, Nola had spent hours wandering these woods, in all seasons and weathers. Judging by today, spring was still her favorite time of year in the Smoky Mountains.

The discreet speed limit signs for the narrow road up to Hawkridge were falling behind faster than they should. Nola leaned forward and put her hand on the front seat, but before she could ask the driver to slow down, he'd already done so. In another moment, the car stopped altogether.

She changed the question. "Is something wrong?"

He turned around in the seat, looking past her through the rear window. "There's a kid back there, hiking along the road."

Nola shifted to follow his gaze. "He's walking oddly. Do you suppose he's hurt?"

"If you don't mind waiting a minute, I'll go and check."

Nola watched as the driver hurried back in the direction they'd just come. The boy stopped as soon as he saw the man approaching. There was a moment of hesitation as they faced each other. Then the driver returned to the car alone.

Nola rolled down her window. "Is he all right?"

Taking off his cap, the man scratched his head. "He's carrying a huge turtle. That's why he's walking weird."

"A turtle?"

"This big." He rounded his hands, indicating a circle at least a foot in diameter. "But he won't talk to me at all." Smoothing his thick gray hair, he replaced his cap. "I guess he's been told not to talk to strange men in cars. My kids and grandkids always were."

"Oh." She looked at the boy again, saw how he bent and twisted his body, presumably to keep hold of a wiggling turtle. With the size of that shell, the animal had to be heavy. "Do you think he would talk to a strange woman?"

The driver looked worried again. "I don't—"

A glance at her watch showed her they couldn't afford much more delay. "Let's find out." She released the door latch, and the driver jumped forward to pull it open for her. Then together they headed back down the road.

The day was warm for March in the mountains, the sunlight strong. A light breeze stirred her hair and cooled her cheeks. Nola stopped about ten feet away from the boy. "Are you okay?"

He nodded. "Yes, ma'am." Dark, silky hair fell

across his forehead and into his hazel eyes. His cheeks and arms were pale and freckled, his jeans, shirt and boots filthy. "Just trying to get this fella home."

The turtle's arms and legs flailed, exposing sharp claws that came closer to scratching the boy's arms. Its head and tail poked out of and retreated into the shell, and with each move, the boy was forced to adjust his balance to compensate.

The driver glanced at the woods surrounding them. "Couldn't you just put him down in the woods some-where along here?"

"I found him down on the highway—he almost got run over twice before I could pick him up. He needs water, and someplace safe. We have a pond near the house I think he'll like."

"How far do you have to go?" Nola asked.

"Coupla miles."

"What are you doing this far from home? And on Hawkridge property? This is private land, you know."

"My dad works there. He'll help me take Homer to the pond."

"I've never heard of homer turtles." Nola glanced at the driver, who shrugged.

"Me, neither." The boy flashed her an amused look, displaying a deep dimple near each corner of his mouth. "This is *Terrapene carolina carolina*. A common box turtle. Homer's what I'm going to call him. After the Greek poet."

"Well, then, if you're okay…" Nola turned toward the driver. "We should be on our way."

He touched the brim of his hat. "Yes, ma'am." But

then he looked at the boy again. In a low voice, he said, "I hate to leave him alone out here."

Nola looked at her watch again. "He's perfectly safe."

"Two miles is a long way to walk for a little kid."

She took a deep breath. "You want to give him a ride?"

"If you wouldn't mind, ma'am. Since we're going to the same place."

She looked back at the boy. "Would you like a ride to the school?"

He grinned. "Sure!" But then his face fell, as he appeared to reconsider. "Uh… I'm not supposed to ride with strangers."

Nola stared at him, not sure what to do next. "Well. Um…I'm not exactly a stranger. I'll be teaching at Hawkridge for the next few weeks. I'm Nola Shannon."

Relief brought out another dimpled grin. "I'm Garrett. If you're a teacher, then it'll be okay." He marched forward, his squirming burden held in front of him. "Let's go. My arms are getting tired."

"You don't want that animal in the car with you," the driver told Nola as they followed the boy. "It's filthy."

She nodded. "We'll put him in the trunk."

With the trunk of the limousine open, however, Nola experienced second thoughts. So, evidently, did the turtle's rescuer. "Homer might get hurt if a suitcase fell on him," he said. "It would be good if we had something safe to put him in." He gazed at her luggage. "Can we take the stuff outta that little bag and put Homer in there?"

The driver gasped. "Absolutely not!"

But Nola, looking at the boy's worried face, said, "I guess so." *It's just my Louis Vuitton lingerie case.*

With her underwear tucked into a different bag and Homer installed in French leather luxury, she and Garrett got into the backseat of the car. Still shaking his head, the driver restarted the engine and resumed their course.

"Would you like something to drink?" Nola opened a small refrigerator.

"Awesome." The boy sat forward, his eyes wide. "Is this your car?"

"I rented it at the airport. Soda, juice or water?"

He pointed to a can of soda. "Have you got food, too?"

At the touch of her fingers, a sliding panel above the refrigerator revealed crackers, nuts, chips and candy. "Be my guest."

"Oh, wow."

He'd barely stopped chewing long enough to breathe before the car emerged from the shady forest into bright afternoon light. Just ahead, the road split into a circular drive leading to the front door of the Victorian mansion which housed the Hawkridge School.

Nola chuckled. "I'd forgotten—it looks like a castle, doesn't it?"

Garrett nodded and swallowed at the same time. "Some of the girls call it Hawkwarts. You know, like the Harry Potter books?"

"There is a resemblance." The brick and stone house possessed its share of round, pointed-roof turrets, plus acres of diamond-paned glass in the casement windows and hundreds of feet of iron railing around porches and balconies. The overall effect should have been forbidding, like the setting of a gothic novel. But after twelve years away, Nola had the strange impression that she'd been on a long, difficult journey and had now, finally, come home again.

The car stopped on the paved drive in front of the house. As Nola emerged onto the cobblestone drive, girls' voices floated through the open doorway of the main entry hall, competing with the birds twittering in the trees.

Garrett scrambled out behind her and went immediately to the rear of the car. "I need to get Homer to some water."

Lifting the lid of the trunk, the driver said, "I'll deliver your bags, Ms. Shannon. Just have someone to tell me where I should put them."

She turned to the driver and extended her hand. "I will. Thank you for everything. You've been a good sport."

He grinned. "Hey, it's not my suitcase that turtle's traveling in."

Nola rolled her eyes. "I don't want to think about it."

Garrett started up the wide granite steps, but then hesitated and turned back to wave at the driver. "Thank you for the ride," he said, his cheeks flushed. "Me and Homer woulda had a long walk."

The driver returned a two-fingered salute. "No problem."

Nola joined Garrett on the steps. "Where do you think you'll find your father?"

"There he is now. Dad! Hey, Dad!"

Garrett ran to the circular staircase and started up,

lugging the suitcase with him, dodging the girls who lounged on the steps. "Come see what I found, Dad. It's the coolest box turtle ever!"

Somewhere out of sight, a man said, "A box turtle, so early in the spring?" His accent was soft, Southern, the tone low and masculine. "I guess this warm spell has brought them out of hibernation."

His voice hadn't changed, and Nola would have recognized it anywhere. The years rolled back and she was eighteen again…

She was standing at the foot of the staircase on a hot late-August afternoon, when a gorgeous guy wearing jeans and a navy sports jacket stepped through the front door. He slipped his backpack off his shoulder, looked in her direction and grinned.

"I'm Mason Reed," he said in a delicious Southern drawl. "The new physics teacher. And you are…?"

In love, *Nola had answered silently.* Totally and forever in love. With you.

* * * * *

Love Inspired
HISTORICAL

Powerful, engaging stories of romance, adventure and faith set in the past—when life was simpler and faith played a major role in everyday lives.

See below for a sneak preview of
HIGH COUNTRY BRIDE
by Jillian Hart

Love Inspired Historical—love and faith throughout the ages.

Silence remained between them, and she felt the rake of his gaze, taking her in from the top of her wind-blown hair, where escaped tendrils snapped in the wind, to the toe of her scuffed, patched shoes. She watched him fist up his big, work-roughened hands and expected the worst.

"You never told me, Miz Nelson. Where are you going to go?" His tone was flat, his jaw tensed as if he were still fighting his temper. His blue gaze shot past her to watch the children going about their picking up.

"I don't know." Her throat went dry. Her tongue felt thick as she answered. "When I find employment, I could wire a payment to you. Rent. Y-you aren't thinking of bringing the sheriff in?"

"You think I want *payment?*" He boomed like winter thunder. *"You think I want rent money?"*

"Frankly, I don't know what you want."

"I'll tell you what I don't want. I don't want—" His words cannoned in the silence as he paused, and a passing pair of geese overhead honked in flat-noted tones. He grimaced, and it was impossible to know what he would say or do.

She trembled, not from fear of him, she truly didn't believe he would strike her, but from the unknown. Of being forced to take the frightening step off the only safe spot she'd known since she'd lost Pa's house.

When you were homeless, everything seemed so fragile, so easily off balance, for it was a big, unkind world for a woman alone with her children. She had no one to protect her. No one to care. The truth was, she'd never had those things in her husband. How could she expect them from any stranger? Especially this man she hardly knew, who was harsh and cold and hard-hearted.

And, worse, what if he brought in the law?

"You can't keep living out of a wagon," he said, still angry, the cords still straining in his neck. "Animals have enough sense to keep their young cared for and safe."

Yes, it was as she'd thought. He intended to be as cruel about this as he could be. She spun on her heel, pulling up all her defenses, and was determined to let his upcoming hurtful words roll off her like rainwater on an oiled tarp. She grabbed the towel the children had neatly folded and tossed it into the laundry box in the back of the wagon.

"Miz Nelson. I'm talking to you."

"Yes, I know. If you expect me to stand there while you tongue lash me, you're mistaken. I have packing to get to." Her fingers were clumsy as she hefted the bucket of water she'd brought for washing—she wouldn't need that now—and heaved.

His hand clasped on the handle beside hers, and she could feel the life and power of him vibrate along the thin metal. "Give it to me."

Her fingers let go. She felt stunned as he walked away, easily carrying the bucket that had been so heavy to her, and quietly, methodically, put out the small cooking fire. He did not seem as ominous or as intimidating—somehow—as he stood in the shadows, bent to his task, although she couldn't say why that was. Perhaps it was because he wasn't acting the way she was used to men acting. She was quite used to doing all the work.

Jamie scurried over, juggling his wooden horses, to watch. Daisy hung back, eyes wide and still, taking in the mysterious goings-on.

He is different when he's near to them, she realized. He didn't seem harsh, and there was no hint of anger— or, come to think of it, any other emotion—as he shook out the empty bucket, nodded once to the children and then retraced his path to her.

"Let me guess." He dropped the bucket onto the tailgate, and his anger appeared to be back. Cords strained in his neck and jaw as he growled at her. "If you leave here, you don't know where you're going and you have no money to get there with?"

She nodded. "Yes, sir."

"Then get you and your kids into the wagon. I'll hitch up your horses for you." His eyes were cold and yet they were not unfeeling as he fastened his gaze on hers. "I have an empty shanty out back of my house that no one's living in. You can stay there for the night."

"What?" She stumbled back, and the solid wood of the tailgate bit into the small of her back. "But—"

"There will be no argument," he bit out, interrupting her. "None at all. I buried a wife and son years ago, what was most precious to me, and to see you and them neglected like this—with no one to care—" His jaw ground again and his eyes were no longer cold.

Joanna didn't think she'd ever seen anything sadder than Aiden McKaslin as the sun went down on him.

* * * * *

Don't miss this deeply moving story,
HIGH COUNTRY BRIDE,
available July 2008
from the new Love Inspired Historical line.

Also look for SEASIDE CINDERELLA
by Anna Schmidt,
where a poor servant girl and a wealthy merchant
prince might somehow make a life together.

REQUEST YOUR FREE BOOKS!

2 FREE NOVELS PLUS 2
FREE GIFTS!

American ★ Romance®

Heart, Home & Happiness!

YES! Please send me 2 FREE Harlequin American Romance® novels and my 2 FREE gifts (gifts are worth about $10). After receiving them, if I don't wish to receive any more books, I can return the shipping statement marked "cancel." If I don't cancel, I will receive 4 brand-new novels every month and be billed just $4.24 per book in the U.S. or $4.99 per book in Canada, plus 25¢ shipping and handling per book and applicable taxes, if any*. That's a savings of close to 15% off the cover price! I understand that accepting the 2 free books and gifts places me under no obligation to buy anything. I can always return a shipment and cancel at any time. Even if I never buy another book from Harlequin, the two free books and gifts are mine to keep forever.

154 HDN EEZK   354 HDN EEZV

Name _____ (PLEASE PRINT) _____

Address _____ Apt. # _____

City _____ State/Prov. _____ Zip/Postal Code _____

Signature (if under 18, a parent or guardian must sign)

Mail to the **Harlequin Reader Service:**
IN U.S.A.: P.O. Box 1867, Buffalo, NY 14240-1867
IN CANADA: P.O. Box 609, Fort Erie, Ontario L2A 5X3

Not valid to current subscribers of Harlequin American Romance books.

Want to try two free books from another line?
Call 1-800-873-8635 or visit www.morefreebooks.com.

* Terms and prices subject to change without notice. N.Y. residents add applicable sales tax. Canadian residents will be charged applicable provincial taxes and GST. Offer not valid in Quebec. This offer is limited to one order per household. All orders subject to approval. Credit or debit balances in a customer's account(s) may be offset by any other outstanding balance owed by or to the customer. Please allow 4 to 6 weeks for delivery. Offer available while quantities last.

Your Privacy: Harlequin is committed to protecting your privacy. Our Privacy Policy is available online at www.eHarlequin.com or upon request from the Reader Service. From time to time we make our lists of customers available to reputable third parties who may have a product or service of interest to you. If you would prefer we not share your name and address, please check here. ☐

HAR08R

™Silhouette®

SPECIAL EDITION™

NEW YORK TIMES
BESTSELLING AUTHOR

DIANA PALMER

A brand-new Long, Tall Texans novel

HEART OF STONE

Feeling unwanted and unloved, Keely returns
to Jacobsville and to Boone Sinclair, a rancher
troubled by his own past. Boone has always
seemed reserved, but now Keely discovers a
sensuality with him that quickly turns to love. Can
they each see past their own scars to let love in?

*Available September 2008
wherever you buy books.*

Harlequin American Romance is
celebrating its 25th anniversary
just in time to make your
Fourth of July celebrations
sensational with Kraft!

MEXICAN LAYERED DIP

Prep time:	Total:	Makes:
10 minutes	1 hour 10 minutes (incl. refrigerating)	5 cups or 40 servings, 2 tbsp each

1 pkg (8 oz) PHILADELPHIA Neufchatel Cheese, 1/3 Less Fat
than Cream Cheese, softened
1 tbsp TACO BELL® HOME ORIGINALS® Taco Seasoning Mix
1 cup TACO BELL® HOME ORIGINALS® Thick 'N Chunky Salsa
1 cup drained canned black beans, rinsed
4 green onions, chopped
1 cup KRAFT 2% Milk Shredded Reduced Fat Cheddar Cheese
1 cup shredded lettuce
2 tbsp sliced black olives
3 pkg (13 oz each) baked tortilla chips

(Continued on next page)

MEXICAN LAYERED DIP (continued)

BEAT Neufchatel cheese in medium bowl with electric mixer until creamy. Add seasoning mix; beat until well blended. Spread onto serving plate.

LAYER remaining ingredients except tortilla chips over Neufchatel cheese mixture; cover.

REFRIGERATE at least 1 hour before serving. Serve with the chips.

Kraft Kitchens' Tips

Jazz It Up:
Garnish with chopped fresh cilantro.
TACO BELL® and HOME ORIGINALS® are trademarks owned and licensed by Taco Bell Corp.

Each Harlequin American Romance book
in June contains a different recipe from
the world's favorite food brand, Kraft.
Collect all four to have a complete
Fourth of July meal right at your fingertips!

For more great meal ideas please visit
www.kraftfoods.com.

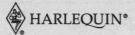

HARLEQUIN®

American ★ Romance®

COMING NEXT MONTH

#1217 SMOKY MOUNTAIN REUNION by Lynnette Kent
The State of Parenthood

The last time Nola Shannon saw Mason Reed was at her high school graduation. Twelve years later she still carries a torch for the handsome teacher—now a widowed father. And Mason's certainly never forgotten *her.* He and his young son need someone special in their lives. Could the lovely, caring Nola be that someone?

#1218 HANNAH'S BABY by Cathy Gillen Thacker
Made in Texas

It's the happiest day of her life when Hannah brings her adopted baby home to Texas. But what would make the new mother *really* happy is a daddy to complete their instant family. And Hannah's friend Joe Daugherty would make a perfect father. He just doesn't know it yet!

#1219 THE FAKE FIANCÉE by Megan Kelly

What's a man to do when his mother wants him to have a family so badly she ambushes him with blind dates? Hire the caterer to be his fiancée, that's what. His mom is thrilled, but will Joe Riley and Lisa Meyer's pretend engagement become the real thing?

#1220 TRUST A COWBOY by Judy Christenberry
The Lazy L Ranch

When Pete Ledbetter's granddad decides to find Pete a wife, the bachelor cowboy has no choice but to get his own decoy bride-to-be. He looks no further than his family's Colorado dude ranch. After a summer romance, he knew he was compatible with chef Mary Jo Michaels. But after their summer breakup, he knew winning back her trust would be nearly impossible....

www.eHarlequin.com